DANNY ORLIS

AND

FRITZ MCCLOUD, HIGH SCHOOL STAR

DANNY ORLIS

AND

FRITZ MCCLOUD, HIGH SCHOOL STAR

BERNARD PALMER

Danny Orlis and Fritz McCloud, High School Star
© 2023 by Bernard Palmer
All rights reserved. First edition 1968.
Second edition 2024.

Scripture quotations from The Authorized (King James) Version. Rights in the Authorized Version in the United Kingdom are vested in the Crown. Reproduced by permission of the Crown's patentee, Cambridge University Press.

Cover image: Adobe Firefly
Character illustrations: John Ball
Editor: Jon D. Fogdall

Aneko Press Youth

www.anekopress.com

Aneko Press, Life Sentence Publishing, and our logos are trademarks of
Life Sentence Publishing, Inc.
203 E. Birch Street
P.O. Box 652
Abbotsford, WI 54405

JUVENILE FICTION / Religious / Christian / Action & Adventure
Paperback ISBN: 979-8-88936-044-5
eBook ISBN: 979-8-88936-045-2
10 9 8 7 6 5 4 3 2 1
Available where books are sold

CONTENTS

CHAPTER 1

FRITZ VOLUNTEERS

It was a bright, early September afternoon in Fairview, Minnesota. The sun was bathing the quiet little town with a warmth that would not be present in a few short weeks. Fishermen were still rushing to the lakes at every opportunity and here and there a group of boys was playing baseball or tossing a football around.

Fritz McCloud was as interested in football as any other broad-shouldered high school junior. He had been keeping in shape all summer and when the first practice was called, he went out eagerly. It had been apparent almost from the beginning that he would make the starting lineup.

This particular afternoon, however, he had completely forgotten football as he approached Danny Orlis' home and knocked.

"I was just going by and saw that you were home,

Danny," he said, "so I thought I'd stop and talk with you if you've got a couple of minutes."

"Sure thing. Come on in and sit down." Danny's smile was contagious. "I might even be able to spare you three or four minutes."

The high school junior crossed the living room and sat down on the couch. For several minutes they talked about a number of things. Danny was interested in the football team and their prospects for the coming season, and wanted to know how things had gone at camp that summer. Fritz answered his questions, but there was something about his manner that made it clear he was concerned about other things. Danny waited quietly until Fritz spoke again.

"I–I suppose it was unthoughtful of me to stop and talk with you tonight," he said, a new intensity taking hold of him as he continued. "But when I saw you were home I–I felt that I just had to."

Danny leaned forward and lowered his voice so those in the other part of the house could not hear what he was saying. "You don't have to apologize for coming to see me, Fritz," he replied. "You're welcome at our place any time. I'm sure you know that." He paused momentarily. "If you'd like to talk with me privately, we can go into my study."

Fritz shook his head. "It's nothing like that. I just wanted to talk with you about young people's at church. You and Kay are going to be sponsors again this year, aren't you?"

Danny could scarcely cloak his surprise. The McCloud boy had usually come to young people's if he hadn't had something else to do, but that was about as far as it went. He had never seemed particularly interested. In fact, he had always acted as though he couldn't care less about what was going on.

The young missionary pilot looked up at him. "Why, yes," he answered. "As far as we know, we'll be helping with the young people's program again this fall. Why?"

Light gleamed in the boy's eyes, and when he spoke his voice was alive and vibrant. "The last couple of weeks I've been doing a lot of thinking about the kids out at school. Danny, we've got to do something to reach them for Christ."

Danny nodded. "That's the reason Kay and I have been working with the kids at church and have our high school Bible club. We've been very concerned about winning them for the Lord."

There was a short silence.

"That's why I came over to see you." Fritz paused and a faraway look came into his eyes. "When I get to thinking of all the chances I've missed to witness to the gang, I get so upset I can hardly stand it. I think some of them would accept Christ if we approached them in the right way."

"I'm sure that's true, Fritz. Is there something you'd like to see us add to the program at church?"

The young guest shook his head. "What would I know about planning programs?" he asked. "I just came over to tell you that I want to do something to help, but I don't know what." He swallowed hard. "I thought I'd stop and tell you that if you need someone to do something – anything at all – I want you to call on me."

"I'll do that. Thanks." Danny could contain himself no longer. Curiously, he stared at his visitor. "You weren't especially interested in Christian things last spring, Fritz," he went on. "Would you mind telling me what happened?"

Fritz grinned, but only for a moment.

"You knew that Connie and I went to Bible camp this summer, didn't you?"

The pilot nodded. "If I remember correctly, I think Jim was there the same week."

"Jim was there, all right. He was so busy with Connie he didn't know I was around. But he was there. Only, after he and Connie left, I stayed on. To tell you the truth, I spent half the summer there."

"I guess I knew that, too. Kay and I saw you around the grounds a couple of times when we were out there."

Fritz' voice rose. "I got interested in that program of Bible memorizing and witnessing out there." The comers of his mouth tightened. "I felt as though I had to stay for the rest of the course. I didn't have enough money for it, but I talked the camp director into letting me hang around."

He tugged thoughtfully at the lobe of his ear.

"I hadn't been there very long until I saw that my Christian life didn't amount to very much. I was saved, all right, but that was about as far as it went.

I didn't really care about the other kids I knew and what happened to them. In fact, now I wonder if I cared very much about God."

"I'm afraid most of us are that way. We're saved and glad we are, but that's the end of it. We never actually do very much for the Lord."

Fritz scooted forward on the couch.

"I think that's the thing that's been buggin' me so much since I got home. I want to do something to help win the kids at school for Christ!"

* * * *

Later that night Jim Morgan and Connie left the McCloud home and walked slowly out to the curb.

"I didn't know you had the car tonight," she said. "I thought we'd be walking."

"Not tonight. This is a special occasion. I talked Danny into letting me have his car."

"That's nice."

He opened the door for her and went around to the other side and got in. It was several moments before either of them spoke.

"What time does your train leave tomorrow, Connie?" he asked, at last.

"Oh, didn't I tell you? I won't be going by train after all. The folks decided to take me over there."

"That's right. I forgot." He drove slowly down Main Street and turned in the direction of the highway.

This was the time he had been dreading all summer. At first it had seemed like a bad dream, but one that would happen only in the far distant future. Now, however, it was here. After tonight they would be separated. And who knew when they would get together again – or if they ever would? It was enough to take any joy he might have out of going to school.

Finally, Connie spoke. "What time are you leaving for Cedarton?" she asked.

"On the noon bus."

She expelled her breath thoughtfully. "I should be happy and excited about going away to college," she said after a time, "but I'm not. I wish you were going to school with me."

He nodded. "I feel the same way. And I wish you were going to school in Cedarton with me."

The brief silence seemed unbearable.

"It's such a long time until Thanksgiving vacation."

"It'll go fast." He spoke with an assurance he did not feel. "Besides, we'll be writing to each other once in a while."

Her smile was weak and fleeting. "I hope we write more than that."

"You can count on it. I'll probably be writing you so much you'll be sick of hearing from me."

She settled back in the seat, and it was a moment or two before she spoke again.

"You have my address, don't you, Jim?"

"I sure have." He reached for his billfold. "Don't worry. You'll be hearing from me."

She eyed him shyly. "You say that now, but you'll probably forget all about me when you get to CBI and see all the girls there. I'll just be someone from back home."

"Oh, no you won't!" He spoke firmly. "You know that's not true." He turned onto the highway and accelerated to the legal speed limit. "If anyone does any forgetting, it'll be you. You'll forget all about me. You'll see all those fellows at college and you won't even remember that there was anyone back home."

"Jim!" She was close to tears. "You know that isn't true."

"That's the way it works lots of times."

She dabbed at her eyes with a tissue.

"I'm sorry," he replied. "I was just joking."

"I don't even like you to joke that way."

It was a long while before they spoke again. Jim broke the silence, changing the subject abruptly.

"Fritz was at the house today," he said.

Connie nodded. "When he got home, he told us that's where he'd been. He said he felt as though he had to see Danny and talk with him."

"When I got home from work, they were in Danny's study praying for the kids out at school."

Connie's face wrinkled thoughtfully. "Something has happened to Fritz lately, Jim," she said. "He's never been that way before – so interested in spiritual things, I mean."

"He told Danny that he finally had his eyes opened to the way a fellow should live. He said he got into that Bible memorizing program out at camp and started witnessing, and it really changed his life."

There was a certain longing in Connie's young voice. "You know, when I see him the way he is now, it makes me ashamed of my Christian life."

Jim's eyes narrowed. "I know just what you mean. When Danny was talking about Fritz at the table tonight, I was terribly ashamed of the way I've been living and how little I have actually accomplished for Christ."

CHAPTER 2

FIRST LETTER

The evening before the first football game of the season, Fritz was getting into his uniform. Ordinarily there was a great deal of banter as the squad dressed for a game, but on this particular evening the fellows were strangely quiet. Millard was twice as large as Fairview and always fielded an excellent team. Most of the sports editors in the area had picked Millard to sweep the conference. And at their first game the week before Millard's team had shown what a powerhouse they were by overrunning their opponent with ease.

Kit Landry was sitting on the end of a bench in the locker room lacing his football shoes when Fritz went over and sat down beside him.

"Hi, Kit," he said happily. "How're you doing?" His friend looked up, scowling. "OK, I guess." Fritz began to put on his football shoes, softly whistling a few bars of a favorite hymn. Kit frowned.

"If you want my advice, you'd better quit that whistlin' and start prayin'."

"How come?"

"We're goin' to get the beating of our lives tonight."

"Aw, come off it. They haven't beaten us yet."

"They haven't beaten us yet," Kit repeated, standing and tying up his shoulder pads. "But don't be so sure it's not goin' to happen. Have you read last night's paper?"

Fritz grinned. "Why read the paper?" he echoed. "That's just some guy's opinion of what's going to happen. We're going to give him something to take back in the next issue. We'll teach that Millard outfit a few things about football."

Kit picked up his helmet and started for the door. "I sure wish I was as confident about it as you are."

Millard won the toss and elected to receive. On the first play after the kickoff the tailback took the ball on their own ten-yard line and started forward, gathering blockers as he went. Fritz came charging in, eluding one defensive man, and diving for the ballcarrier. He hit him so hard the ball squirted out of his hands and Kit Landry fell on it. The crowd went wild as Fairview took possession on the Millard twelve-yard line.

Fritz surveyed the situation quickly and called a play around left end. Dale Cuyler, the fullback, growled his disapproval.

"Come on, Fritz," he protested. "Let me carry the ball. I'll go through those guys like nothing."

The youthful quarterback acted as though he hadn't even heard him. "Number 65."

The fullback swore savagely. Fritz' head snapped up, eyes flashing.

"OK, Cuyler," he ordered sternly. "There's not to be any swearing on this team."

Anger twisted the brawny fullback's face.

"And just who's goin' to stop me?" he demanded. "If I want to swear, I'll swear and I won't be askin' your permission, either!"

Evenly the youthful quarterback's gaze met his and held there.

"As long as I'm running this team there's not going to be any swearing on the field. Clear?"

Dale's lips started to form a word, but he checked himself. In the face of Fritz' firm stand the burly fullback backed down. "Just let me carry the ball," he muttered. "That's all I ask."

"I'm calling the plays, too," Fritz reminded him. He moved toward his position to break up the huddle. "Number 65."

The fullback's face was white and drawn as he took his place for the play Fritz had called.

Kit took the ball, faked a hand-off to Fritz and sliced around left end. One desperate tackler got his fingers on him, but he managed to twist away to get down to the five-yard line. Millard expected another end around, but Fritz called for a reverse with Dale carrying the ball. The big fullback eyed him curiously but said nothing. On the play he got through to the Millard one-yard line, and on the next play he punched the ball across for the first touchdown of the evening. Their place kicker came in to make the score 7 to 0.

There the score stood until the dying moments of the final quarter when Millard scored a touchdown on a long run. They lined up hurriedly, electing to run for a possible two points rather than to try for a tie. Fritz broke through to nail the ball carrier in his tracks before the final gun sounded.

He was one of the last to shower and dress after the game. Almost everyone else had gone when he left the locker room and went down the corridor to the side door of the senior high building. Dale was waiting for him in the shadows.

"Hey, Fritz," he called out. "Can I talk to you a minute?"

"Sure thing." Curiously, Fritz followed him. "What's on your mind?"

Dale was having trouble expressing himself. "I–I can't make you out, that's all," he blurted at last.

Fritz eyed him uneasily. "Why? What've I done?" The other boy stared at him. "You mean you don't know?"

Fritz shook his head. "I gave you a bad time in the huddle," Dale began, "and I figured that as soon as you got a chance you were going to squeal to the coach and get me in plenty of trouble. But what did you do? A play or two later you had me carry the ball. You even let me score." The expression on his face changed. "I don't get it at all."

"That's easy," Fritz said, laughing. "I figured you were the best one to carry the ball at that particular time. That's all."

The other boy stared at him. Once or twice, he tried to speak but could not. Then, impulsively, he thrust out his hand. "I won't give you any more trouble. You can count on that."

Fritz stared after him until he disappeared into the darkness. A warm feeling of satisfaction swept over him. He thanked God for it. He had stood firm in his testimony, but God had helped him to be fair. Now he had won Dale's respect. Maybe he would be able to win him for Christ. That night he knelt beside his bed and prayed for a long while for his fullback friend, that he would take his stand for God.

* * * *

At Cedarton Bible Institute Jim Morgan went down to the school post office to check his mail. The day's distribution had just been finished and most of the student body was there, checking their boxes, laughing, and talking excitedly.

Jim's room mate, Quinn Regan, was standing nearby, a couple of letters in his hand.

"There's nothing for you, Jim," he said, laughing pleasantly.

"Don't kid yourself."

"I know how these things go. She's forgotten you already."

Jim opened his box and took out several letters, noting quickly that there was one from Connie. Quinn saw it too, glancing brazenly over his shoulder.

"Hmm. She did write to you after all. What's the matter with her, Jim?" he asked. "Hasn't she wised up to you yet?"

Jim ignored his good-natured bantering. "Come on. Let's get in line for lunch. I'm about starved." "You mean you think more of your stomach than you do a letter from your best girl? What kind of a guy are you?"

"The letter will wait. If we miss out on dinner, we go hungry until tonight."

"Wait until she finds that out. There won't be any more letters."

"Besides, I want to read it in private."

"You can read it in private. Go off in a comer and open it quick to see if her delicate little heart still beats for you."

"I can wait."

"Of course, it could be one of those 'Dear John' letters. You know how they go, don't you? 'I am so sorry, my dear, but I know I'm not good enough for you. So please send back my picture by return mail so I can give it to Joe. '"

"Stop. You're breaking my heart."

Jim wanted to open Connie's letter and read it, but he couldn't. Not with Quinn sitting across from him, that mocking light gleaming in his eyes. He liked his good-natured room mate, but there were times when he wished he would get lost.

It was another half an hour later before Jim was alone and could open his mail in peace. Although there were letters from both Uncle Carl and Aunt Mary, and Danny and Kay, he opened Connie's letter first and read it thoughtfully.

She still missed him, he noted with satisfaction. Either that, or she was trying to kid both herself and him. And she seemed to be very interested in whether he missed her or not. The rest of the letter was filled with talk of the university.

"I certainly wish you had come here to school, Jim," she wrote. "And not only because I miss you so much. Here we get exposed to some of the best teaching you'll find anywhere in the country. I especially enjoy my class in English Lit. The instructor isn't a Christian, but he has a way of provoking thought that is most stimulating.

"A group of us got to discussing his philosophy last night. We kept talking until after midnight. I can't say that I agree with everything he says. In fact, I know I don't. But he does draw some interesting conclusions about life."

"The kids here at State seem to be so much more mature and do so much more thinking than those at home. Did you ever stop to consider what a chaotic world we live in? A few nuclear bombs exploded in the right places around the world and civilization as we know it could be wiped out in a moment of time. It sort of makes you feel, 'What's the use of preparing to do anything? Why place any restraints on your actions or try to accomplish anything? We might just as well have a good time. There's no need to worry about tomorrow. We don't even know if there's going to be a tomorrow.'"

Jim read the balance of her letter and laid it aside thoughtfully. That didn't sound like Connie at all. If it hadn't been in her handwriting, he would have thought someone was putting him on. He got out the letter and read it again. He was just finishing it for the second time when Quinn came in.

"Bad news?" he asked. This time there was no banter in his roommate's voice.

Jim shook his head.

"Not the kind you're talking about. But I don't mind telling you, Quinn, that this letter from Connie bothers me a great deal."

He read parts of it aloud.

"What do you think?" he asked when he finished.

"It sounds to me as though she's being taken in by all this so-called 'advanced thinking' at State."

"That's the way I got it. This sort of talk isn't like Connie at all."

"She is a Christian, isn't she?"

Jim nodded. "She's a fine Christian," he said. "I've always been certain that she had high spiritual standards – as high or higher than mine."

Quinn sprawled on the bed and cupped his hands behind his head. "Secular universities are fine for some fellows," he said, "but a guy from our church back home got excited about that stuff at school in the East last year. He came home for the summer with a long beard and–"

Jim grinned crookedly. "I don't think I'll have to worry about that. I don't think Connie'll come home with a beard."

"No, but it sounds to me as though she's going to come back with some strange ideas unless she gets hold of herself fast."

Jim was very serious. "That's exactly what I've been thinking," he said. "That's what's got me so concerned."

That evening Quinn and Jim had a special time of prayer for Connie, that she would be able to level out and not allow those ideas that were contrary to sound Christian teaching to twist and warp her faith.

CHAPTER 3

ANOTHER VICTORY

The next football game was out of town. The team was excused early from classes and left in the school bus in the middle of the afternoon. Some of the fellows were playing cards in the back of the bus. Some were sprawled in the seats trying to sleep, while still others were talking excitedly about the game they would be playing in a few hours. Fritz McCloud, however, had taken his New Testament from his pocket and was leaning against the window, reading it. Eric Johnson looked up from the card game, saw what he was doing, and snickered.

"What're you doing, Fritz?" he asked, his lips curling in derision. "Are you studying up so you can give us a sermon on the way home?"

Fritz was so engrossed in what he was reading that he didn't even hear him.

Eric snickered again.

"If you want some guys to preach to, I can give you a good list. The fact is, I'm playin' cards with a terrible bunch of sinners right now."

Dale slammed a card on the seat and turned to his companion, eyes blazing.

"Pipe down, Swede," he exclaimed shortly, "and play. It's your turn."

The rangy halfback stared at him.

"What's got into you, Cuyler? You've got no call to get your back up."

"Lay off Fritz!" the fullback retorted. "If he wants to read that Bible of his, OK. That's his business. You don't have to give him any static about it."

At the mention of his name Fritz stopped reading momentarily and glanced back.

"Somebody talking to me?"

Eric laughed. "I was just going to give you a prospect list of real sinners for you to work on," he said. "You can put Dale Cuyler's name at the head of the list."

Crimson sneaked up into the powerful fullback's face.

"I don't need a new list," Fritz said easily. "I've already got one."

That seemed to stop Eric. His cheeks flushed. By this time everyone in that end of the bus was listening.

"Am I on it?"

"Do you think you ought to be?"

Everybody laughed, breaking the tension.

When they reached their destination Dale called Fritz to one side. He was easily the biggest man on the squad.

"If those guys keep pestering you, Fritz," he said guardedly, "just let me know. I'll clobber them."

"It doesn't bother me to have them talk that way," he said. His grin was disarming.

"Well, it bothers me."

"Forget it, Dale." There was a note of command in his voice. "We can't be fighting among ourselves and play together the way we should. We've got a football game to win."

"But I was just trying to get them off your back, Fritz."

"I know, and I appreciate it, but it doesn't bother me at all. So let's skip it. OK?"

Dale pushed his cap back on his head. "I can't figure you out."

A new confidence had taken over the Fairview eleven as they ran out on the field to start the Stanton game. They won the toss and, electing to receive, took the kickoff on their own eleven-yard line.

Dale and Kit came thundering over to give Eric protection and Fritz threw a key block downfield to knock out the nearest defensive man. Gathering speed, the ballcarrier snaked across the twenty-yard line, avoided two tacklers, and bulled his way to the thirty-two before being brought down by two or three dark-shirted Stanton linemen.

"OK, guys! Let's go!" Fritz' voice shrilled above the roar of the crowd as he led the team out of the huddle.

He started to call signals when he saw that the Stanton secondary was out of position and was wide open for a short pass into the flat. Without hesitation he barked out a change in the play number. The backfield shifted quickly.

Fritz took the ball from center, faked a plunge over tackle and dropped back to lob a soft pass over the line to Ken Pierson's eager, grasping fingers. Stanton pulled him down, but not before he had reached their forty-nine-yard line for a first and ten.

On the first play of the next series of downs, Dale carried the ball for a two-yard gain. With a second and eight, Fritz called for a long pass that fell just beyond Vince Turman's fingertips. The next was an option play. He planned on throwing again, but his receivers were covered. Faking the ball to Kit who came up fast, Fritz sidestepped one tackler and burst through the hole in the line and dashed into the open. It happened so fast that few on the field even knew what was going on until Fritz sped past the last would-be tackler and crossed the goal line standing up.

Fairview scored again in the second quarter and once in the fourth to make the final score 21 to 0.

The big fullback came over to Fritz as they trooped toward the bus after showering and changing into their street clothes.

"That was a great game, Fritz."

The corners of his mouth lifted into a crooked grin. "We did all right, at that."

"*You* did all right," Dale continued. "If it hadn't been for you, we'd have been lucky to have squeaked by with a single touchdown."

"I wouldn't say that."

"I would. You sized up those guys on every play."

"I had a lot of help out there, Dale," Fritz replied seriously. "There were ten other fellows playing their hearts out all the time. Just remember that. If it hadn't been for the rest of you, I couldn't have done a thing. That's for sure."

* * * *

The following afternoon Fritz stopped by the Orlis home.

"Hi, Kay," he said. "Is Danny around?"

"He isn't here yet, but he should be back any time. Won't you come in and wait for him?"

He glanced at his watch. "I guess I've got time to wait for a little while."

A moment or two after he sat down in the living room, DeeDee Davis came in.

"Hello," she said, smiling shyly.

"Hi."

Before he could say anything else, Doug Davis started into the living room from the kitchen. The instant he saw Fritz he stopped; his lithe body stiffening.

"Kay!" he spoke in a hoarse whisper. "Is that who I think it is?"

"I don't know." She came to the door, quizzically. "Who do you think it is?"

"Is that Fritz McCloud?" Awe tinged his young voice.

"Yes, why?"

Doug's amazement grew.

"You mean it's *the* Fritz McCloud?" he persisted as though he could not quite believe that it was Fritz who was sitting in their living room.

"I don't know whether it's *the* Fritz McCloud or not," Kay answered, "but he's the only Fritz McCloud that I know."

"I didn't think he'd ever come over here to see us." Doug's voice trembled. "Do you know he's won just about every football game for Fairview since he moved here?"

"This is the Fritz McCloud who plays football," Kay said. "I've heard him and Danny talking about the games. He's the quarterback, I believe."

Doug nodded. "And DeeDee's sitting in there talking to him!" There was incredulity in his voice.

"You can go in and talk to him if you'd like," Kay said.

At that moment Danny came in and took Fritz into his study. When they were gone, Doug called his sister into the other room and talked with her guardedly.

"Do you know who you were talking to?" he demanded.

"Sure."

"Who was he?"

"Connie's brother."

Doug's eyes widened. "Connie's brother!" he exclaimed. "Connie's brother! That's all you can say about the greatest football player in the whole state of Minnesota." He sighed at her ignorance.

"It doesn't make any difference to me whether he plays football or not," she said, "as long as he's nice."

Doug went into the other room shaking his head. He'd like to go in where Danny and Fritz were and get introduced to the star quarterback. He'd like to get where he could just see him, but he couldn't do that. Danny had taken Fritz into his study so they could be alone. He knew better than to break in on them.

* * * *

Danny closed the door and had his young guest sit down.

"Now," he said, "what can I do for you?"

Fritz leaned back and crossed his legs. "You remember, I was telling you about Dale Cuyler the other day and asked you to pray for him?" Fritz began.

The missionary pilot nodded.

"He's the fullback, isn't he?"

"That's right. I've been talking to him a lot lately and I think he's going to start coming to church and young people's with me."

"Good," Danny exclaimed. "I'm glad to hear that. But, of course, we have been praying for him. We can expect God to work."

"At least he said he'd go," Fritz continued. "But I'm not entirely sure whether he meant it or not. I–I just wondered if you'd pray for him with me."

They bowed their heads right where they sat and asked God to bring Dale to the services and to help him see his need for a Savior. When they finished, Fritz' face was dark with apprehension.

"Thanks, Danny."

"You don't have to thank me. It's a real privilege to have you come and ask me to pray with you for one of your buddies."

Fritz acted as though he wanted to leave but could not immediately.

"I wish there was some way we could get hold of all the guys on the team." The boy's great concern darkened the laughter in his eyes. "They're a great bunch of guys, Danny. You couldn't find a better squad anywhere. And I really like them." He shook his head. "But they don't know Christ as their Savior."

"Kay and I will be praying that you'll be able to witness to them, Fritz, and to bring quite a few of them to Christ."

"Thanks, Danny. Thanks a lot." This time he opened the door. "You know, it makes a fellow feel better just being able to come over here and talk with you."

"I'm glad of that. Feel free to come any time."

"I'll do that."

Danny went to the front door with him and stood there until Fritz was gone. Then he turned slowly back to the kitchen.

"You know, Kay, there aren't many boys with the spiritual depth and perception Fritz McCloud has."

CHAPTER 4

TRIPLETS' TROUBLES

Dale Cuyler was in Sunday school and church the following Sunday. Fritz had called him on Saturday night to make sure.

"I can stop by for you at about 9:30 tomorrow morning, if you'd like," he suggested.

"You won't have to do that. I only live a couple of blocks from the church. I'll be there."

"Swell. I'll be waiting for you on the front steps."

"OK."

There was a large crowd for both services that morning, but Pastor Reeves saw Dale and after the worship service he singled out the newcomer and spoke to him warmly. He recognized Dale from his picture with the football team and called him by name.

"We're so glad to have you with us this morning, Dale," he said. "Do come back again."

The boy seemed surprised that he had been recognized and spoke about it. "How did you know my name?"

"I've seen you play football." He looked the brawny fullback over. "I'd sure hate to be playing on defense and have to try to tackle you."

Dale grinned.

Someone else spoke to the minister just then and he had to turn away. Fritz and Dale went on out the door and down the steps.

"I'm sure glad you came this morning, Dale," Fritz said.

"So am I." There was genuine interest in his voice. "I've been to church a few times in other places, but I didn't know there was such a friendly church in town as this one."

"How about going with me again tonight?"

His companion hesitated.

"I'd better not make any promises about tonight, Fritz," he replied. "I'm not sure whether I can make it. But I'll go with you again sometime. I'll promise you that."

That night Pastor Reeves called Fritz aside after the evening service.

"I was talking with Danny today, Fritz," he said, "and he tells me that you're the one who got Dale Cuyler to come to church today."

"I've been working on him," Fritz acknowledged. "But I wasn't sure whether he'd be here or not until I saw him this morning."

Pastor Reeves nodded. "I want you to know that I really appreciate it. I wish all our church members would be as concerned about their friends and would try to get them to services. If they did, I'm sure we'd see some big changes in Fairview."

* * * *

The Davis triplets found that going to a regular school was entirely different than taking lessons by correspondence. For one thing they found the discipline of sitting in classes all day most difficult. And the fact that they no longer had a personal tutor to give them guidance through every step of a difficult lesson caused a certain amount of trouble. They could go to their teachers at school for help, if they wanted to, but for some reason they didn't. Their grades dropped off a great deal.

Doug and Del acted as though it didn't matter much to them. However, it bothered DeeDee considerably. She brought her books home every night and, spreading them out on the kitchen table, she studied until it was time to go to bed. Kay was always there to help her with those things she had difficulty in understanding. Even then she found it hard to maintain the sort of grades she had by correspondence.

"I don't know what's the matter with me, Kay," she said on more than one occasion. "I've tried and tried to get good grades, but I just can't do it." In spite of herself her discouragement showed through.

"I wouldn't be so upset if I were you. You've been taking all your subjects by correspondence up until now, and it isn't easy to make the change." She went over and sat down beside DeeDee, putting her arm about her. "I had to do the same thing, so I know all about it."

"But Miss Leslie said that studying by correspondence is harder than in a classroom," the girl countered. "If that's true, then we ought to be getting better grades than we did when we were studying at home."

"Perhaps it is harder for some people to study by correspondence," Kay said, "but you haven't known anything else. That's why you're having so much trouble right now. It won't be so bad when you learn how to study this way."

DeeDee shook her head doubtfully, as though she would never learn it.

"Now, what's giving you the most trouble tonight?"

"Everything!" She burst into tears. Kay gathered her into her arms and let her cry.

Doug and Del weren't worrying about their grades, however. They found football and playing with the other kids at school too exciting to spend time doing homework. They raced through their lessons during school so they could play as soon as class was dismissed. When Danny and Kay asked them about their studies they always had their assignments finished. Danny, especially, questioned them at length.

"Are you sure they're done?" he asked.

They both nodded vigorously. "Oh, sure. They're done. We finished early today."

"That's right," Doug added. "I didn't even have enough to keep me busy during the last half of arithmetic class."

"Neither did I," Del said, "so I went over my answers twice, just to be sure I had them right."

Danny broke in. "You know, I can't figure this out," he said, looking from one to the other. "It seems strange to me that you two never have any homework to do and DeeDee always does. How do you account for that?"

Doug and Del glanced at each other blankly.

"I don't know," Doug muttered.

"Neither do I," Del said. "Maybe she works slower than we do."

"I don't believe I've ever seen any of your school papers. Have you got any of them in your room?"

They shook their heads.

"I just haven't been bringing any home, Danny."

"Neither have I. I–I didn't think that you'd be interested."

"Well, we are interested," the pilot said. "We're very interested in your homework. I'd like to have you bring your papers home when the teacher gives them back to you."

The boys agreed quickly. But that was before they saw the next papers that they got back. Doug flushed as he looked at his.

"What'd you get?" he wanted to know.

Del did not answer him directly.

"I didn't do very well."

"Neither did I."

They left the school and walked slowly down the sidewalk. The new development was disconcerting.

"Miss Leslie wrote on my paper," Del said at last.

"She wrote on mine too." Doug handed his paper to his brother.

"She wrote the same thing on mine," Del went on. "She said that I could do much better if I applied myself."

There was a brief silence.

"I don't know what that teacher expects out of a fella, anyway. Nobody could be expected to get all of those assignments."

"I'll bet she flunked half the class."

"That's just about like her. Girls are her pets. They can get away with anything. But boys!" Doug wrinkled his nose distastefully. "I sure wish we had somebody else for a teacher."

"Me, too."

"If we'd stayed in Texas, I'll bet we'd have been studying by correspondence."

Del nodded. "Aunt Carmen would sure be a lot easier on us than that Miss Leslie."

They crossed the street and turned in the direction of Danny and Kay's.

"You know what I think? I think Miss Leslie's got it in for us. I'll bet she doesn't like us because we're missionary kids."

There was a short silence.

"I don't think that's it," Del went on. "I think she got mad at us for something else."

They were almost home before either of them said anything more.

"Danny's sure going to be mad when he sees these papers," Del observed. "He's going to blow his stack!"

Doug squinted thoughtfully at the dirt-smudged papers in his hand. "Do you think he'll remember to ask for them?"

Del pulled in a long, deep breath. "I hope not, but I sure wouldn't bet on it. He told us that he wanted us to be sure and bring them home. I don't think he's going to forget about them."

Doug looked at his paper again.

"If Miss Leslie liked us, it would be different," he said. "We'd have good grades. But she's not being fair. She gave us low grades because she's got it in for us and wants to get us into trouble."

Del thought about that for a minute. It did seem logical, he reasoned. The teacher was always bawling out him or Doug and she almost never scolded DeeDee. That just went to prove that she played favorites.

"Since it's that way," he said, "we really wouldn't be doing anything wrong by not showing these papers to Danny, would we?"

"I guess not."

They tore their papers to shreds and stuffed them in the trash barrel as they came by the back of the Orlis home.

Del and Doug waited uneasily for Danny to come home that evening. They were both greatly relieved when Kay told them he would not be back until the next day.

"He had to fly a new missionary up to his station in northern Ontario," she said.

That was just the reprieve they needed. The next day they saved the best papers Miss Leslie handed back to them. And it was a good thing as far as they were concerned. As soon as Danny got home, he asked about their studies.

"How'd the lessons go this week?"

"OK," Del answered.

"Did you bring home your papers?"

"I've got mine." Doug fished a paper from his pocket and handed it to Danny. Del did the same.

Danny looked them over carefully.

"You both got D's," he said. "That's not very good."

Doug spoke up defensively. "That's because Miss Leslie doesn't like us," he countered. "It doesn't make any difference how hard we study. She won't give us good grades."

"That's right," Del added. "She's that way with all the boys."

The corners of Danny's mouth tightened. "Come off it, fellas," he said, "If you get a D, it's because you earned a D."

They would have argued with him, but they saw that it was useless.

Danny looked over their papers carefully.

"Take a look at the mistakes you've made on these papers," he said, at last. "I think Miss Leslie was very generous in giving you a D. If I'd been teaching this class, I'd have failed you both."

Neither boy answered.

"From now on I want to see you fellows doing homework the way DeeDee does, and we're starting this tomorrow night. OK?"

"I guess we can," Doug said, shrugging his shoulders in resignation, "but that means we'll have to sit around in school half the time doing nothing, doesn't it, Del?"

"Yeah. And Miss Leslie will scream her head off about that."

"Maybe you'd better work a little more thoroughly and use your school study time, too."

The following night the boys brought their books home and studied for a time.

"Well, that's that," Doug said, "I'm finished." He closed his books and pushed them aside.

"I'm done, too."

Danny looked up from his newspaper. "Are you sure?"

"Sure, I'm sure. I did most of my studying in school and I could have gotten this done too, but you said I had to bring home some work to do here."

Danny went over to check their papers, but the phone rang for him. While he was gone, they put their books away. Del glanced at the kitchen door and leaned toward his brother, whispering softly. "Danny's getting worse than Miss Leslie," he said. "He won't be satisfied until he has us studying all the time. The trouble is, he doesn't want us to have any fun at all."

Doug nodded. "We wouldn't have had to study that way if we'd stayed down on the ranch," he continued. "We could work our correspondence courses and have plenty of time for ourselves. Uncle Clarence would have let us ride fence and help take care of the calves and things like that. It wouldn't be studying all the time."

"You can say that again," Del replied. "Sometimes I wish we were back there."

"So do I."

The following morning Attorney Corwin called Danny and asked him to bring Kay down to his office that day.

"I've got some papers for you to sign," he said.

"Have you been in touch with the judge?"

"I've had correspondence with the judge and also with the Roper attorney."

"Is everything in order?" Danny tried to keep his voice calm but did not succeed very well.

"As far as I've been able to determine, everything's moving along very nicely. Mr. Roper talked personally with the judge to tell him that he and his wife want no part of the triplets under any circumstances. That, of course, removes the last legal hurdle."

Danny sighed his relief. Somehow, he had been concerned that the Ropers would change their minds in spite of the fact that Carmen had flown up to Minnesota with the triplets. Kay was waiting beside the phone when he hung up.

"What has he found out?" Fear laced her voice.

Briefly he repeated his conversation with the attorney.

"So it appears to be only a matter of time and a few more dozen papers to sign before the kids are legally ours."

Kay went back to the kitchen table and sat down. "That's certainly an answer to prayer." "You can say that again."

The silence hung heavily between them.

"There's one problem the triplets are going to have to face before long, Danny."

"What's that?"

"They'll have to decide whether to keep their own family name or to take ours."

CHAPTER 5

TANGLE WITH DAD

Saturday evening when Fritz came home from his part time job his dad was sitting at the kitchen table cleaning his twenty-two rifle.

"Hi, Dad." He took off his jacket and hung it in the closet. "Been hunting?"

"Nope," Mr. McCloud answered. "But I'm getting ready to go out and plink at a few rabbits. I haven't had a chance to get out this fall."

Fritz went to the refrigerator and got himself a glass of milk.

"I've been thinking some of going out myself. Kit and Swede went last Saturday and did all right."

"How about going with me?" Lester McCloud suggested. "I'm planning on going tomorrow morning." Fritz' young face clouded. "Tomorrow?"

"Right. We'll get Mom to fix a lunch for us if you want to. That way we can stay out all day – just you and me."

"But tomorrow's Sunday."

"I know that," his dad said off-handedly. "It isn't going to hurt anything for us to take a day off this once. We're in Sunday school and church almost every Sunday. The pastor can't expect anything more from us."

Fritz sat down across from his dad, his youthful face serious.

"I'd like to go hunting with you Dad, but not tomorrow."

"Why not?"

"I–I just don't feel right about going hunting on Sunday."

His father's cheeks colored, and ice crept into his voice.

"This must be something new for you, Fritz. I've never heard you say anything like that before. In fact, I can remember plenty of times when you were after me to go fishing or hunting, or do something else that would take us away on Sunday. And it didn't seem to bother you much."

The boy toyed uneasily with his glass.

"That was before camp, Dad." He swallowed the lump that had grown in his throat. "At camp this summer I made the decision to put God first in my life."

The muscles in the older man's mouth tightened.

"And you don't think I'm doing the Christian thing by going hunting tomorrow. Is that right?"

"I didn't say that, Dad."

"You'd just as well have said it. That's exactly what you meant."

"No, it isn't, Dad." He tried desperately to explain. "I don't have any right to judge what you do or don't do. And I'm not trying to find fault with you."

"Maybe that's what you say, but that isn't the way it sounds to me." Lester McCloud pushed his chair back from the table angrily and stood up. "Well, you don't have to worry about my 'tempting' you to do wrong. I won't ask you to go hunting with me again."

"Dad!"

Lester McCloud stormed into the living room and dropped heavily to a chair. Fritz' mother, who had been watching television, looked up.

"Oh," she said, "I thought you were Fritz."

"He's out in the kitchen."

She caught the anger in his voice. "Is there something wrong?" she asked.

"No, there's nothing wrong." Anger smoked darkly in his eyes. "That kid of ours has just been preaching to me, that's all."

"Fritz?" she echoed incredulously.

"Yes, Fritz! I wanted him to go hunting with me tomorrow morning and he gave me a lecture as though I'd broken all the Ten Commandments."

Mrs. McCloud took a deep breath and exhaled wearily. There had been other occasions when her husband and son had had words, but never over spiritual things. It was almost a minute before she spoke.

"What did Fritz say that made you so angry, Lester?" she asked.

"He said–" He started quickly but stopped. Getting to his feet he went over and switched off the television set. "He said that he didn't feel right about going hunting on Sunday."

She waited patiently, but he did not continue. At last, she spoke again.

"Is that all he said?" she asked.

"He said that he'd make a decision to follow God's will for his life when he was out at camp this summer. He said that he didn't feel he could go hunting with me because of that." Lamely his voice trailed away.

She started to speak but checked herself.

"OK." His irritation grew. "Go ahead. Say it!"

"Say what?"

"Say what you're thinking – that it isn't what Fritz said to me that made me angry – that it was the Lord speaking to me and I didn't like it because I enjoy going hunting on Sunday and didn't want to change."

Her gaze met his and when she spoke her voice was scarcely above a whisper. "Isn't that the truth?" she asked quietly. "Isn't that the real reason you got so furious?"

Anger twisted his usually mild features. "I just don't like the idea of having my own son tell me that I'm not living the way a Christian should live, that's all."

She did not answer him.

"There isn't anything wrong with going hunting on Sunday or missing church once in a while to go to a ball game or on a picnic," he continued defensively. "I work hard all week. And I'm not like most men. I even have to work most Saturdays and once in a while on an evening during the week. A fellow can't go to church all the time. He's got to have a little relaxation." As he spoke, rage thickened his voice. "I–" He stopped suddenly.

"You don't have to convince me that it's all right for you to do anything you want to do on Sunday," his wife said. "I'm not the final judge on that sort of thing."

He whirled on her, his temper flaring. "That's right! I don't have to convince anybody that what I'm doing is all right! If I want to go out for a little enjoyment on Sunday, I'll go! And I won't ask you, or Fritz or anyone else if it's all right. Is that clear?"

He stormed into the bedroom and slammed the door behind him.

Mrs. McCloud had been interested in the television program before her husband came in. Now, however, she did not turn the set back on. She sat motionless in the chair, except for her fingers which were working nervously. There had been a change in Fritz, a terrific change in the past few weeks. A number of people had mentioned it.

Not that Fritz had ever been a bad boy. He had been good, even before he accepted Christ as his Savior. And afterward his life was such that other parents pointed to him as a model for their own children. But the big change had come about since he took the Bible memorizing course out at camp.

There was a boldness about his Christian testimony that she had never noticed before. And a kindliness in his manner that seemed to set him apart. He had a concern for others that few who had been Christians for fifty years attained.

The finger of guilt shouldn't point at her husband alone, she knew. He wasn't the only one in their family who was careless about the Lord's Day. In fact, she had understood what was bothering him because it was also a knife in her own heart. She couldn't even remember the number of times picnics, ball games, or stock car races had kept their family away from church on Sunday. And she had been the one to suggest the outings, fully as often as her husband and the kids. The blame was hers as much as it was Lester's.

Fritz came in presently, talked with her a moment or two, and went on to his room. After he left, she didn't even know what she had said to him. She was still sitting in the same position when her husband returned almost an hour later.

Lester McCloud came back into the living room slowly, as though every movement was an effort of will. Momentarily he stood beside the door, looking down at his wife.

"Vivian?" There was a different tone in his voice.

"Yes?"

There was also a different look in his eyes, a look she had never seen before.

"Is Fritz still here?"

"He went to his room a few minutes ago."

"I've got to talk to him," he blurted.

"He isn't angry with you, Lester," she said. "And he wasn't trying to criticize you or find fault. He was only trying to explain why he couldn't do what you wanted him to."

"I know that." He sat down on the edge of a straight-backed chair and leaned forward. "I really wasn't angry with Fritz. I was angry with myself. The Lord was using him to convict me about my careless attitude toward the Lord's Day."

There was a long, painful silence.

"The truth of the matter is," he continued, "that we haven't been living dedicated Christian lives. We've been careless and have let our love of enjoyment and pleasure creep in to move us away from God."

"I've been sitting here thinking the same thing, Lester. We need what Fritz got out at Bible camp this summer."

"I know." His voice broke and it was a moment before he could go on. "I settled it on my knees in the bedroom just now. "That's what I want to see Fritz about. I want to tell him what happened and to ask his forgiveness."

* * * *

At school Del and Doug continued to treat their lessons with careless indifference. They studied at home when Danny and Kay insisted on it. The rest of the time they rushed through so they would be able to play or fool around. They were both very surprised when the school principal sent for them to come to her office. Apprehensively they looked up at their teacher.

"You mean we're supposed to go and see her right away?" Doug asked, curiously.

"That's right," Miss Leslie replied.

"But we're supposed to be in math class."

"You'll be excused from math."

"Can't we see her after school?" Del wanted to know. "We could see her just as well then."

The boys remained seated.

"You'd better go now," Miss Leslie repeated. "Miss Kirby doesn't like to be kept waiting."

"Wh-what does she want to see us about, Miss Leslie?" Doug asked.

"I'm sure she will tell you."

"We haven't done anything," Del broke in.

"Then you don't have anything to worry about."

"But–" He still could not hide his nervousness.

"Miss Kirby wants you to go to her office right away." There was an authoritative ring to the teacher's voice that made them both know that time had run out. They left the classroom and started up the corridor to the principal's office. Outside the door they paused.

"What do you suppose she wants to see us about?" Doug whispered uneasily.

"Search me."

"Maybe we could sneak out the back way and go home without going in to–to talk to her."

"That wouldn't do any good," Del said. "We'd have to come back tomorrow and she'd get us then." He took a deep breath. "And we'd really be in a jam."

Doug started to reach for the door. "Do–do you suppose it would do any good to–to pray about this?"

His brother shrugged his shoulders. "I don't know. You remember what Dad used to say about God not helping us to do things that are wrong."

"But we don't even know what we've done. How could it be wrong?"

"We'd better go in or she'll be out here and have us by the ear!"

Reluctantly Doug opened the principal's office door. There was Danny sitting near Miss Kirby's desk and from the look on his face he wasn't very happy! The boys felt the color drain from their cheeks.

CHAPTER 6

PRINCIPAL'S OFFICE

"**D**anny!" Doug exclaimed. "What are you doing here?"

Miss Kirby answered for him.

"Mr. Orlis is here because I asked him to come." Her eyes were arresting and cold. "I wanted him to be present at this meeting."

"I–I–" Doug swallowed hard.

The principal looked from Danny to the white, drawn faces of Doug and Del, and back again. "Mr. Orlis, I asked you to come in so that you can hear exactly what I am going to say to the boys, and they can hear what I am going to say to you."

Doug and Del squirmed uncomfortably. They thought they should be talking – trying to defend themselves – but they didn't know what to say.

"I don't know whether you are aware of it or not, Mr. Orlis," the principal continued, "but Del and Doug have been doing very poor work since the school term started."

"I'm a little surprised to hear this," Danny replied. "Both Kay and I have been asking them how they've been doing, and they've always assured us that everything was going along very well."

The boys squirmed.

"Their grades have been far from satisfactory. Far from satisfactory." She pulled in a long, deep breath. "I have talked with the teachers about it a number of times. At first, we thought it was probably caused by the difficulty they were having in making the change from correspondence courses to regular classes in school. We know there is a certain amount of trauma in making such a change."

Hopefully Del glanced at his brother. It wasn't much of an opportunity to wriggle out of this, but it was worth a try.

"That's right," he said. "It's been hard for us to learn to study in class after taking all of our other courses by correspondence."

Miss Kirby stared icily at him.

"As I was saying," she went on, "we thought at first that their low grades were because of the change in their method of study. Then we realized that their sister had exactly the same problem, but she has been able to keep her grades up satisfactorily. In fact, she is doing very well in her studies. Exceptionally well."

Del and Doug scowled darkly but didn't dare to say anything.

"I'm glad you've called this to our attention, Miss

Kirby," Danny said. "Kay and I are very much concerned about the triplets' grades. We'll do everything we can to help get them up where they belong."

"The boys will have no difficulty, I'm sure." She paused, the muscles about her mouth tightening. "Providing they put in the necessary time studying."

"We'll see that they get their homework finished," Danny assured her, "and on time."

She smiled. "Thank you, Mr. Orlis. We always find it so much easier to do our best for our students when the parents are understanding and cooperative."

Once outside the office Del and Doug eyed Danny hesitantly. Finally, Del elected to speak.

"It isn't as bad as Miss Kirby tried to make it sound, Danny." In spite of himself and his effort to sound firm and confident, there was hesitation in his voice. "We just happened to get some low grades in a couple of tests, and she got all shook up, that's all. If we study a little extra for the next couple of weeks, we'll have our grades up where they ought to be."

"Yeah, that's right," Doug continued. "All we've got to do is to study a little extra for a few days and we'll have it made."

Danny opened the car door and got in. They slid into the front seat beside him.

"I'm glad to know that you can bring your grades up with a little extra study," he said. "In that case you can probably get on the honor roll with the amount of studying you're going to be doing."

Their dark eyes widened.

"What?"

"Studying every school night and two hours on Saturday night ought to put you both on the honor roll."

They stared at him as though they couldn't believe what he was saying.

"You–you mean we're going to have to study every night?" Doug asked.

"That's right," Danny told him. "You're going to have to study every night, except Sunday."

"For how long?"

"A couple of hours."

Horror clouded Doug's face. He couldn't have felt more hurt had Danny insisted that they study all night.

"You–you've got to be kidding! You–you don't expect us to study for two whole hours every night, do you?"

"I certainly do," Danny said. "And what's more I'm going to see that either Kay or I hold a watch on you to be sure that you put in that much time."

"But–but we've got time to study in school," Del countered. "We–we wouldn't have enough work to keep us busy for two whole hours every single night."

"Then you can use the rest of the time in review. From what Miss Kirby said you can stand it."

There was a brief silence.

"We–we'll wear our eyes out with all that study-ing." Doug's face was somber. "You wouldn't want to have us make our eyes so weak we'd have to wear thick glasses, would you?"

Del broke in hopefully. "That's right," he said. "If you make us study so much, we'll have to wear glasses and won't be able to go out for football or anything."

"That's one risk we'll just have to take."

The boys settled back in the seat, staring at one another in their misery.

At home DeeDee was waiting for them, concern dulling her eyes. As soon as she could, she got them off to one side.

"What happened?" she asked. "What did Miss Kirby want with you?"

Doug scowled at her. "What makes you think something happened?"

"I waited and waited for you when school was out, but you didn't come, so I went back." She lowered her voice to a whisper. "Then I saw both of you in Miss Kirby's office with Danny. I–I've been so scared I–" Her voice trailed away.

"We're really in a mess," her brother told her angrily. "And it's all your fault."

Her cheeks blanched. "My fault?" she echoed. "What did I do?"

"You did all that studying and got good grades, that's what you did."

The boys both faced her accusingly.

"Yeah," Del added, "and now we're in a jam because of it."

They told her what had taken place.

"And now they say we've got to get good grades too."

DeeDee looked from one to the other indignantly.

"It's your own fault!" she said firmly. "It's not mine. You could do like I do. You could study."

Doug shook his head. "If that isn't just like a girl!" he exclaimed. "For cryin' out loud!"

Danny hadn't been fooling about the nightly study periods, although the boys had been hoping against hope that he had been. As soon as they finished their evening devotions after dinner, he noted the time.

"All right, fellows," he said. "It's 6:45. Time for you to go to your room and get to studying."

Del hesitated, trying to size up the situation. "Right now?"

"Right now."

"For two whole hours?"

"For two whole hours."

Sighing his dejection, he got to his feet and shuffled off to their bedroom. Doug followed him, just as miserable.

Kay turned to Danny. "I forgot to tell you that we got a letter from your folks today," she said.

"What did they have to say?"

"They're coming to Fairview to spend their wedding anniversary with us."

His face beamed. "Boy, that's great. A real family reunion."

Kay was silent momentarily.

"That's what I'd like to make it," she said.

"What do you mean?"

"I've been thinking about Kent and Jill ever since

we got your folks' letter this morning. I wish they could come home too."

"Sounds like a good idea."

"Do you think the school will let them?"

"I don't know, but we can sure find out. I'll drop them a line this evening."

"If they could come, everything would be just wonderful."

He went over and put his arm about her slender waist.

"You still miss those kids, don't you?"

"I've missed them more today than I have any time since they left." She paused momentarily. "I don't know why, but I haven't been able to think of anything else since the mail came."

Danny kissed her lightly on the cheek.

"We'll have to see what we can do about getting them home for a few days."

At school Fritz and the fellows on the football squad were preparing for the toughest game of the season. There had been touches of overconfidence on previous Friday nights, but not this time. Everybody on the team was keyed up as they filed into the locker room to dress.

Dale came over and sat down beside Fritz, untying his shoes.

"Have you seen the size of that Hanridge line?" he asked uneasily.

Fritz laughed. "They're probably asking one another about the size of our line," he said.

"But we don't have anyone as big as the Hanridge

center and their tackles. They outweigh us by at least twenty pounds."

"The bigger the fellow is, the bigger the hole when he's taken out."

Dale shook his head. "I wish I was as sure we're going to win as you are, Fritz."

"Oh, we're going to win, all right. It's going to be a tough game, but we'll take 'em."

The coach came in just then and called them to attention.

"Hanridge is big and tough." He paused significantly. "But so are we. It's going to be a hard-fought game, but if we play the kind of football we're capable of playing, we can beat them by two touchdowns."

When he finished, they ran out on the field and warmed up.

Fairview won the toss and elected to receive. Ordinarily the kickoff went to Dale or Kit, but this one was short, and wobbly and almost went out of bounds. Fritz dashed over and stooped to pick it up, but hesitated for an instant. When it bounded along the sidelines, he snared it with both hands and twisted to avoid a tackler who was charging in fast.

He didn't see the other Hanridge tackler, even when the fellow hit him. Suddenly he was thrown to the ground, his leg doubling under him. Sharp excruciating pain shot from his knee up into his hip!

His head swam! Nausea swept over him in a black, reeling flood!

CHAPTER 7

INJURED IN ACTION

For the space of a moment or two pain surged through Fritz' powerful young body in great, driving blows. Sweat pearled his forehead and moistened the sallow whiteness of his cheeks. He clenched his fists and grimaced weakly as he fought for breath.

Dale was the first Fairview football player to bend over him.

"Fritz!" he cried, his voice tightening. "Fritz! What happened? What's the matter?"

It was only with effort that the injured boy could speak.

"My knee–my knee!" he managed.

The members of both teams were crowding about, staring down at him. By this time the football coach realized that something more had happened than Fritz being shaken up. He ran out on the field and pushed his way through the circle of players to kneel beside the young quarterback. Even as he looked at him, he saw that Fritz had been painfully injured.

"What's the trouble?" he asked.

"I–I really fixed things this time, coach." The boy spoke weakly.

The football coach examined his injured knee.

"That sure doesn't look very good. How does it feel?"

"Not so bad." His gaze sought that of the coach. "I'll be able to play again, won't I? This knee won't keep me from playing, will it?"

The coach did not answer him. "Will it?"

"We'll have to see about that."

"What do you think?" A new desperation crept into the boy's voice.

"I wouldn't say that it would keep you from playing." The coach tried to sound sure of himself, but he spoke without conviction. "I've seen a lot of bad knees that fellows have been able to play on. The doctor can usually do a lot for an injury like this."

There was a brief silence. The boys parted silently to let a local physician approach the player on the ground. He knelt beside the coach and looked at Fritz' knee carefully.

"What do you think, doctor?"

"It's not good. I can tell you that much without an X-ray. We'll have to get pictures of it to be sure, but my opinion is that it's as bad as any I've seen in the last several years."

The ambulance came out on the field while the crowd watched in silence. The attendants put Fritz on a stretcher and drove away with him. The injection the doctor had given him began to ease the pain. He relaxed slightly.

One of the attendants noticed the change that began to come over him. "Feel a little better?" he asked.

"I–I guess so."

"Don't you know?"

The muscles in the boy's face tightened. "I–I'm letting the guys down," he muttered. "They need me out there."

"They'll get along all right without you."

"But you don't understand! This is the toughest game of the season!"

"Hanridge has a good team. We have to say that for them."

"I'll say they've got a good team." Fritz' voice rose. "And I would have to get banged up so I can't help the guys!"

The ambulance attendant started to reply but thought better of it and remained silent.

The doctor followed Fritz to the hospital and examined Fritz' knee carefully.

"What do you think, Dr. Walsh?" the boy asked, concern growing in his voice. "How is it?"

"You've got a bad knee – a very bad knee."

"I'll be able to play football again, won't I?"

The physician hesitated. "I'm not sure I can answer that question yet, Fritz. We'll have to take X-rays, and even then, we may have to wait and see how the knee responds to treatment."

He finished his examination, made some notes on the injured boy's chart, and left the room. As the door closed behind him Fritz shut his eyes and began to pray.

* * * *

Danny had wanted to go to the football game that evening but had been delayed at the airport until it was too late. When he got home the triplets had already gone to the football field, but Kay was still there.

"I thought you wanted to go to the game, Kay," he said.

"I did." Her smile flashed. "But I decided against it. I didn't want to go without you."

He crossed the kitchen floor and sat down near the table.

"You look especially happy tonight. How come?"

"Can't I look happy without a special reason?" she asked.

"Sure. You always look happy. But you can't fool me. There's something up that makes you feel a lot better than usual." A mock anger clouded his face. "Now come on. Out with it!"

"I wasn't going to tell you yet," she teased. "I was going to surprise you."

"Now, that wouldn't be nice."

"But I changed my mind."

"You'd better. If you know what's good for you, you'd better."

She came over and sat down across from him.

"I might as well tell you. You won't give me a moment's rest until I do." Her smile broadened. "I had a phone call this afternoon, Danny."

"It must have been a good one to bring a smile like this."

"Oh, it was. The superintendent of the School for the Blind called."

"The kids can come?" he asked.

"They can come. And that's not all." Her eyes were dancing merrily. "He said that Kent is making remarkable progress."

"That is good news."

"He says that Kent has adjusted better than most blind youngsters of his age, and that he's at the head of his class. Isn't that wonderful?"

Danny nodded. "It certainly is. But the thing I'm most concerned about is his spiritual growth. Did he say anything about that?"

She paused.

"Not exactly. But he did say that Kent is no trouble at all. He's cooperative and understanding, and a leader among the boys."

"That certainly doesn't sound like Kent," Danny replied. "He must be making spiritual progress too, or he wouldn't have changed in so many ways."

"That's what I figured."

"No wonder you're so happy." Danny sighed deeply. "When you think about that, it makes you wonder what would have happened to Kent if he'd kept going the way he started out."

Kay's eyes were serious. "I can't even stand to think of what it would have been like," she said. "Perhaps it took a tragedy like this to wake Kent up."

"That's true."

They went into the living room and sat down. Danny picked up the paper and glanced at the headlines.

"Did we get any mail today?"

"Nothing except a couple of advertisements."

"I thought we'd be hearing from the folks by now," Danny said.

"I wrote and told them that you'd be flying up to the Angle to pick them up the last of the week, but we haven't had an answer yet."

He noted the calendar. "Come to think of it, there's hardly been time enough for a letter to get up to the Angle and an answer to get back. They don't have the same sort of mail service that we have."

"I guess you're right." Kay rubbed her throat thoughtfully. "We're just so anxious to see them that the time seems to drag."

Danny nodded. "It's going to be good to have everybody together again," he murmured. "It's been so long I can hardly remember it."

* * * *

In the football stands after Fritz' injury, Mr. and Mrs. McCloud got to their feet and made their way out. They found their car in the parking lot and drove to the hospital. Dr. Walsh was just completing his examination when they reached the emergency room.

"How is he, doc?" Lester McCloud asked.

"He's got a badly injured knee."

Mrs. McCloud broke in, her voice tremulous. "It isn't anything serious, is it?"

The doctor smiled reassuringly. "If you mean, is he in critical condition, no," he said. "But he is painfully hurt and may have a long period in the hospital and at home before he'll be able to go back to school."

"What about his sports career?" Fritz' dad wanted to know. "Will he be able to play football and basketball again?"

The doctor did not reply immediately. He studied Fritz' chart for a minute or two. When he looked up his face was serious.

"I wish I could answer that with some degree of confidence that I'm right," he said. "I've seen knees worse than this that healed rapidly, and the fellows were able to play again as though they'd never had an injury. On the other hand, I've seen knees that haven't been injured as badly as this one keep a fellow from playing anything more strenuous than croquet."

Lester's eyes clouded. "That's what I've been afraid of," he said.

"Now I don't want you to read something into what I've said that isn't there. Actually, we can't be sure of anything regarding Fritz's knee until we've taken X-rays. We'll have to see how he responds to treatment." He paused again. "But it is a definite possibility that his athletic participation is over and he'll have to be prepared for that."

Mrs. McCloud broke in quickly. "That doesn't matter at all to me. I don't care if he isn't able to look at another football again. All I care about is that Fritz is all right."

Dr. Walsh smiled reassuringly. "There's no question about that, Mrs. McCloud. Now, if you'd like to see him for a few moments, it would be fine."

"Oh, thank you."

She started for their son's room, but her husband restrained her, gently.

"How is he, doc?" he asked. "His spirits, I mean."

"How is he most of the time?" the doctor asked. "Bubbling over. Frankly, he's one of the most remarkable kids I've ever met."

Lester nodded his agreement. "I've felt the same way about him, even though he is my own son."

"Since he got back from spending most of last summer at Bible camp, his whole life has taken on new meaning and purpose," Mrs. McCloud said.

Dr. Walsh eyed her quizzically. It was obvious that he didn't understand what she was talking about.

CHAPTER 8

KENT AND JILL ARRIVE

On Friday night shortly after supper Danny and Kay went down to the bus depot to meet Kent and Jill Gilbert. Kay insisted that they go twenty or thirty minutes before the bus was due, and she sat there glancing uneasily at her watch.

"Nervous?" Danny asked her.

"A little."

"They'll be all right, Kay. Don't be so concerned about them."

"I know I shouldn't be, but I can't help it. I still wish we'd gone after them the way I wanted to."

"But the superintendent asked us not to. Remember? He said that Kent and Jill would be able to manage, and that it would be good for them to take the responsibility."

"I know, but Jill is such a little girl to be taking care of both of them."

There was a short silence.

"She isn't taking care of both of them, Kay," Danny said, speaking softly. "We mustn't forget that God is taking care of them. And He loves them more than we do."

"I'm sorry, Danny." A weak smile tugged the corners of her mouth upward. "I guess that's just the mother instinct popping out."

A minute or two later the bus rumbled around the corner and braked to a stop near the hotel.

"There they are!" Kay cried.

Danny took his young wife by the arm and together they pushed forward. At the same time Jill had stopped on the bus step and raised on tiptoe, scanning the crowd.

"They're here, Kent!" she squealed delightedly. "Danny and Kay are here!"

With care born of long practice she guided him off the bus. An instant later she was in Kay's arms.

Danny took Kent's hand and shook it vigorously. For an instant there was a question on the boy's face.

"Danny?" he asked uncertainly.

"That's right."

"I thought it was you," Kent said, a trace of pride in his voice. "You're the only one I know who shakes hands that way."

"How are you, Kent?"

"Great. Just great. Especially now that we're back here with you."

Danny got their suitcases and they went to the car.

"Is Jim going to be home?" Kent asked.

"He should be here in the morning."

"Good. I'll sure be glad to see him. It's been a long time." He smiled happily. "It's been a long time since we've seen any of you, and we've sure missed you."

"We've missed you, too," Danny told him.

They got into the car and started home.

"Well," the missionary pilot said, "how have things been going with you, Kent?"

Kent hesitated.

"It was sort of rough at first, Danny," he began. "But then I realized that I didn't have to do everything alone. I saw that I could put my trust in the Lord for strength and courage." His face seemed to light up. "You'd be surprised what a difference that made. I began to get along better with the rest of the kids and everything. Even my grades got better."

"Yes, that's the way things go when we put our whole trust in God," Danny said. "He doesn't take our problems away, but He does help us to face them."

There was a long, painful silence.

"You know, Danny," the blind boy went on. "I've been doing a lot of thinking lately about what–what happened to me."

"Yes?"

"If God hadn't stopped me by letting that dynamite cap explode in my face, I–I don't know what would have happened to me. I might have wound up in jail or the reform school or some place like that."

"You weren't running with a very good bunch of kids, that's for sure."

Kent breathed deeply. "I don't think God made me blind to punish me or–or anything like that. I think maybe He just allowed it to happen to me to show me where my stubbornness and love of sin were taking me.

"I get to feeling awfully sorry for myself every once in a while, and all of that, but I–I'd rather be this way and–and be living for the Lord than I would to have my sight and to have kept on the way I was headed."

When they arrived at the house Danny and Kay introduced Kent and Jill to the triplets. The blind boy turned to Del and Doug.

"You guys may not know it, but I'm going to tell you something. You're living with the best people you can find anywhere."

"Oh, we know that already," Doug said.

"Just don't give them a bad time the way I did." Kent spoke as though they were the only ones in the room with him. "And if they tell you to do something, you do it. They're only telling you because they feel it's best for you and because they want you to grow up with a strong Christian testimony."

The boys looked at each other sheepishly.

"I used to get terribly mad at Danny because he gave me a bad time about studying," Kent went on, unaware that he was putting his finger on a very pressing problem. "Don't you do that. Pay attention to what he says. He's only trying to help you."

Del and Doug faced Danny quickly.

"Did you tell him, Danny?"

"Tell him what?"

"You know," Del said.

Danny shook his head. "No, I didn't tell him anything."

"That's right," Kent broke in. "I was just going by what I was like when I–I–" His voice choked momentarily and he had trouble continuing, "when I first came to live here."

Kay changed the subject abruptly. They sat in the living room visiting each other until almost eleven o'clock before she realized what time it was and whisked them off to bed. When she came back into the living room, Danny was still there, staring at the floor.

"Well?"

He looked up, smiling.

"What are you so lost in thought about?"

"I was just sitting here thinking how much we have to praise the Lord for. Kent has made tremendous spiritual progress, hasn't he?"

"You wouldn't even know he was the same boy," she replied.

"He's not only been able to accept his handicap without bitterness, but he's actually grown spiritually because of it."

Kay sat down across from her young husband.

"We have so many things to be thankful for regarding Kent and Jill," she said after a time. "I thought perhaps they would have grown away from us, but they haven't. They seem to be even closer to us now than they did before they went away."

Danny nodded. "It's Christ who's made the change, Kay," Danny reminded her. "He always binds us closer to each other when we give our lives over to Him."

Kay picked up her Bible and fingered it thoughtfully.

"It's going to be so much easier for me to see them go back this time, knowing how well they're doing and that they still love us."

"Yes," Danny said. "They're really our kids, even though they no longer live with us."

* * * *

The following morning Danny went out to the airport while it was still dark, gassed the plane and checked it out. Only then did he go into the airport office to talk with the manager who had come to work minutes before.

"Had any weather reports lately?"

The manager glanced at the teletype. "It's snowing lightly in Minneapolis if that helps you any."

Danny's face darkened.

"What about Warroad and Baudette?" he asked. "Heard anything from that direction?"

He consulted the tape again. "Yes, there are reports from both of them. It's cloudy and very cold, but no snow is falling."

"What's the forecast?"

"For clearing this afternoon."

"Good. You were beginning to get me worried. I was thinking I might have to wait a day or two before going up after the folks."

As soon as it was light enough for Danny to see, he took off and headed north-northwest toward Warroad and Angle Inlet. Unbroken clouds stretched from horizon to horizon and snow, fine as blown sand, ticked the windshield. He switched on the radio and called the Fairview airport.

"It's snowing a little up here," he reported. "Got anything new on the weather? Over."

"Negative. There's nothing happening here. I'll keep you advised if anything comes in. Over."

"Roger. Standing by."

Danny scanned the sky uneasily. There was just a little snow falling at the moment and the visibility was still good. He had flown countless hours in the same kind of weather. Yet, there was something ominous about the weather – something that he couldn't quite put his finger on. It might have been the slate gray of the clouds or the fact that the wind was blowing harder, cutting his air speed, and gobbling fuel. He wasn't exactly sure of the reason for his concern. For an instant or two, however, he fought an almost uncontrollable urge to turn back.

"That's silly," he told himself. "The weather bureau reported clearing skies over a five-state area and a slight warming trend." Perfect weather, the announcer had called it as he listened to the radio that morning before leaving the house.

He kept on course.

Nevertheless, he was relieved with what the airport manager reported twenty minutes or so later.

"The Twin Cities report that the forecast for our area remains the same. Clearing skies and slightly warmer temperatures. The same report holds for Warroad and Baudette. Do you read me, Danny?"

"I read you loud and clear. Thanks a lot. Over and out."

"Roger. Over and out."

An hour later Danny reported his position to the Warroad airport and gave them his expected time of arrival at Angle Inlet.

"Better not waste any time, CG 109," the Warroad airport manager said. "We've got some sticky weather on the way. Over."

Danny caught his breath.

"Minneapolis reports clearing skies and warmer for your area. Over."

"The weather bureau goofed on this one. We've got a blizzard on the way, and the way it sounds, it's a real one. Do you read me?"

Silence.

"Do you read me, CG 109? There's a blizzard moving into our area. Do you read me?"

Danny shook himself. This was what he had been afraid of in spite of the weather report.

"Affirmative. I read you loud and clear. What's this about bad weather? Fill me in. Over."

"It's not snowing here yet, but I just had a phone call from the man in Rosseau. It's snowing hard there with local blizzard conditions and winds gusting to thirty miles an hour. The visibility is zero to a quarter of a mile with a ceiling of two hundred feet."

Danny noted his position. He could turn back, but he was only a few minutes out of Angle Inlet.

"I'm as close to my destination at Angle Inlet as I am to Warroad," he said. "I'm going on. Over."

"Roger. And good luck. Over and out."

The Warroad airport radio went off and Danny was alone. In the few short minutes he had been talking on the radio the snow had increased measurably. It pecked at the windshield and swirled around the sturdy little plane.

Danny looked down.

The ground was blotted out!

CHAPTER 9

SAFE LANDING

Briefly, fright squeezed the breath from Danny's powerful lungs. He was enveloped in a sea of white. A prayer went up from his heart as he checked the instruments once more. He had flown enough in the north in the winter to realize fully the precarious situation he was in.

"Dear Lord," he prayed silently, "help me to know what to do. Help me to find my way down safely."

Once the first spasm of fear passed with his brief silent prayer, Danny was calm. The aircraft was functioning normally. He was thankful for that. He noted the fuel gauges. He still had one full tank and at least a quarter of another tank. That gave him a certain amount of mobility. He could turn and attempt to outrun the storm, if he decided that was best.

The altimeter read two thousand feet. That was much too high for conditions like those he found himself in where he was flying over comparatively flat terrain. Deliberately he checked the compass to be sure that he was still on course, and began to lose altitude.

The snow was as thick and impenetrable as ever, and the sturdy aircraft bucked against the ever increasing wind. Danny was thankful for the instrument flying he had done. In such a storm the instruments could make the difference between safety and disaster.

He switched on his radio and picked up the phone.

"This is CG 109 calling KS2G. This is CG 109 calling KS2G. Come in, KS2G."

There was no answer.

Only static crackled over the receiver. Danny tried again and again, repeating the call letters of the Warroad Airport, but it was no use. He wasn't able to raise the manager. Reluctantly, he put the radio phone aside.

As he edged the aircraft lower, he peered out the window for some sign of the ground. But there was none. He was still wrapped in a cloud of snow.

The altimeter indicated eleven hundred feet when Danny caught a glimpse of something dark below – or thought he did. Pressing his head against the plexiglass he stared downward. The snow was being blown in great clouds, but he did see the black of the forest below.

His heart leaped.

The snow closed in once more, hiding the trees, but the whiteness did not seem to be quite so impenetrable. He continued to lose altitude until he was down to four hundred feet. At that distance above the ground he could make out the shoreline distinctly.

A prayer of thanksgiving on his lips, Danny checked the chart again in a hurried effort to pinpoint his location. He was going to have to get out of the air as quickly as possible, even though it might mean making a forced landing. A blizzard was no time to be flying.

The missionary pilot scanned the shore intently in an effort to pick up a landmark he recognized. For the space of a minute or two everything looked the same. There were no distinguishing features he could recognize. Then, to his right he saw a narrow white slit in the dark of the forest. A creek! And it looked familiar! He turned to the chart.

Sure enough! There was Harrison Creek! He should have recognized it without looking at the map. He had overflown his folk's place.

Danny banked the plane around and headed back along the Angle. Now everything was more familiar. There was the old schoolhouse where he started his education and had so much fun with the other kids and his dog, Laddie. Next, he flew over the summer cabin that belonged to a newspaperman in southern Minnesota. And just beyond was the modest place where his folks lived.

He'd made it. He'd made it!

At that instant, the engine sputtered.

Danny gasped. His hand stabbed for the throttle. The motor caught momentarily and sputtered again.

* * * *

In the Fairview Hospital Fritz was getting restive. He had been hoping to be released, and the doctor acted as though he might be at any time. Yet he kept putting him off.

"How about it?" Fritz asked that morning as soon as Dr. Walsh came in on his rounds. "Are you going to let me go home today?"

"What's your hurry about going home? The football season's over."

"What's my hurry?" Fritz echoed. "I feel as though I've been in here forever. How long has it been? A couple of years?"

"Take it easy. You'll begin to get used to the place after a while."

The boy groaned.

"You mean I've got a lot longer to stay here?"

"I don't know how much longer you'll have to stay, Fritz," Dr. Walsh said seriously. "But I can assure you this much. We aren't going to keep you in the hospital a minute longer than we have to."

Briefly disappointment flickered in the boy's eyes, but he forced it away with a smile.

"If that's the way it is, I guess I'll have to put up with it, but I sure wish I were going to get out. I'm getting tired of being flat on my back."

"I saw your dad in the post office this morning," Dr. Walsh continued. "He tells me you're going to have company today. Somebody very special."

Fritz' eyes lit.

"That beautiful sister of yours is going to be coming up."

"Is she still home?"

The doctor grinned at him. "I didn't say a word."

In the afternoon, his folks and Connie came to see him during visiting hours.

"Hi, Connie," he said, brightening. "I thought you were going back to school this morning."

She shook her head.

"I decided to stay until tomorrow night."

"To see me or somebody else?" he asked, teasing.

Color darkened her cheeks.

"I don't know what you mean."

"Oh, don't try to kid me," he continued. "I know you didn't stick around here to visit me. Jim Morgan's home, too. Or did you think I didn't know that."

She got a chair and sat down. The smile left her young face.

"You'll never know how badly I've felt that you got hurt, Fritz."

He grinned.

"It's all right, Connie." He spoke simply. "Doc says I'm going to get out of the hospital in a little while." He glanced at his parents. "At least before my hair gets gray."

"You can joke about it if you want to," she went on, "but I can't. I think it's terrible."

The injured football player hesitated, as though

uncertain whether he should speak or not. When he finally did his voice was hushed.

"Ever since I got hurt, I've been trying to decide whether to tell you something or not."

"Yes?"

"You won't laugh at me?"

"Of course not," Connie said.

Their parents said the same.

"The night of the game, I got into my uniform a little while before the rest of the fellows, so while I was waiting to go out on the field to warm up, I read my Bible in the locker room."

Connie's eyes widened. "What?"

"I was reading the second chapter of Revelation." He spoke as calmly as though he was telling her about studying for a history test. "The ninth and tenth verses–"

"You were reading your Bible in the locker room?" She paused. "You must be kidding."

"Why would I kid about a thing like that? I read my Bible in the locker room and on the bus lots of times." He continued where he left off. "The ninth and tenth verses seemed to stand out to me." He took his Bible from the stand beside his bed. "Here, I'll read 'em to you."

" 'I know thy works, and tribulations…. Fear none of those things which thou shalt suffer… be thou faithful unto death, and I will give thee a crown of life. ' "

He pulled in a long, deep breath and expelled the air in a thin stream.

"When I got hurt those words seemed to stand out in bright lights over the football field. So, you see, God knows all about this and He has promised to take care of me. What do I have to worry about?"

Connie's face was ashen. "You mean that actually happened?" In spite of herself, doubt tinged her voice. "You mean it was really just that way?"

"I was afraid you wouldn't believe it."

"Of course I believe it, Fritz," Connie assured him. "You've never told me anything before that wasn't true and I know you wouldn't lie about something like this. Only it–it sounds so strange."

"It was strange to me too," he acknowledged. "And very wonderful."

His mother bent over, impulsively and kissed him on the cheek. "You're teaching all of us what it means to live for Christ, Fritz."

The boy on the hospital bed gasped.

"Don't say that, Mom!" He spoke quickly. "I miss the mark so far! I'm no example to anyone."

His sister stared incredulously at him.

* * * *

Danny fought to hold the plane steady in the powerful crosswind as the engine sputtered. It caught momentarily; then died.

Silence gripped the little aircraft, save for the shrieking wind.

Danny took a quick look at his folks' place and decided against trying to stretch his glide to reach it. With a quick, sure eye he surveyed the lake below and headed down. Without power the aircraft bucked and tossed like a glider in the turbulent air.

Lower and lower the plane glided. The pilot's hands tightened on the controls and he brought the aircraft to the proper attitude, fighting the pull of the savage wind. Sweat stood out on his forehead and his hands and shoulders trembled. Would he make it?

The skis slammed against the ice. The aircraft bounced into the air and slammed down again, throwing Danny against the seat belt. There was no time for him to think as he battled to hold the crippled aircraft steady. It was in times like this that his many hours in the air caused him to react instinctively, without thought.

At last, the plane bounced to a halt.

For a moment or two Danny sat behind the controls, breathing heavily. It scarcely seemed possible that he was down safely. Yet – praise God – he was!

The snow-laden wind tore at his clothes and chilled him thoroughly as he opened the cabin door and climbed out onto the snow. Hurriedly he pushed the plane to the nearby shore and tied it down as securely as he could. Once that was accomplished, he examined the skis and legs carefully. He would have to go over them more thoroughly later, but they gave no evidence of any damage.

At last, he straightened and began to plow through the drifting snow in the direction of his home. The wind bent the trees and billowed the new snow high with frantic bursts of energy. He tightened his parka about his throat and leaned forward slightly against the wind. The temperature seemed even colder as he struggled up the bank and among the trees.

It had been years since he had walked over that same stretch of ground to his folks' cabin, but now it all came back in a rush. He remembered everything in breathtaking detail. For a moment it seemed that he was a boy again and had never been away from the Angle.

CHAPTER 10

NEIGHBOR IN NEED

Danny quickened his pace as he plowed through the deep snow to the house where his parents lived. The path to the little log cabin behind the house where his dad sorted the mail had been scooped earlier in the day, but it was drifting full again. In another twenty minutes no one would be able to tell where it had been. Smoke spiraled invitingly from the chimney of the house.

Danny started to open the door but stopped and knocked loudly. For a moment there was no answer. Had it not been for the telltale spiral of smoke he would have wondered if his mother and dad were home.

He knocked again.

"Just a minute!" his dad called from somewhere in the house. "I'm coming!"

At that sound of that familiar voice Danny pushed open the door and stepped inside to see his dad standing there.

"Hi, Dad!" He was grinning widely.

"Danny!"

"It sure is good to see you, Dad!" Danny shook his father's hand as though he hadn't seen him for years.

"We'd given you up when it started to snow," Carl Orlis said. "We figured that you would have turned back."

By this time Mary Orlis had heard their voices and came into the kitchen. For a minute or two everyone was laughing and talking at once.

"We don't have to stand out here, Danny," Dad Orlis said at last. "We might as well go into the living room and sit down."

Mrs. Orlis broke in. "Danny, are you hungry?"

"You know me, Mom," he answered. "I can always eat."

"You two go in by the fireplace," she told them. "I'll fix some sandwiches and tea."

Danny sat down in a rocker before the fire and, leaning back, cupped the back of his head in his hands. His dad sat down nearby.

"It seems like old times to be back here again, Dad," he said wistfully. "You know, I love this place."

"I'm glad to hear you say that. I can tell you this much, it hasn't seemed quite the same since you left."

"I'd like to come back next summer for our vacation and take the triplets to all the good fishing spots Ron and I used to have."

Carl Orlis' smile broadened.

"Now that would be great. It would bring back old times to have the voices of kids around again."

Mary Orlis came in with a plate of sandwiches and a steaming pot of tea.

"We've been looking forward to going down to your place for our thirtieth wedding anniversary, Danny, but Dad and I would really have preferred to have you all come up here, the way you used to come on special occasions."

Danny nodded.

"Kay and I talked about that. We would rather have been up here too," he said, "but we decided that because there were so many of us to get up here, and only you two to get down to Fairview, that it was better to go there."

"With weather like this, I know what you mean," Carl said.

Danny grinned. "It's not only the weather. I had a bit of engine trouble coming in." He told them about the weather forecast, how the storm hit unexpectedly, and how he had been forced down a short distance from the Orlis place.

"Think you can fix it, Danny?"

"I don't know for sure," he said. "I may be able to if it doesn't take any new parts. As soon as it stops snowing, we'll see."

They were still sitting near the fire when there was a loud, authoritative knock at the door.

Startled, Danny jerked erect.

"Who's that?" he demanded.

His dad got to his feet. "Now, if you'll give me time enough to get to the door, I'll see."

Carl Orlis was still several steps from the front door when it was flung open and a broad-shouldered figure hurried in. The man's parka was rimmed with snow and his eyes were wild and staring.

"Mary!" he cried, his voice coarse with fear. "Where's Mary?"

Mary Orlis went over to him quickly.

"What's the matter, Glen? Is there something wrong?"

"It's Carol. She's terribly sick, and Sally and I don't know what to do."

Mrs. Orlis spoke calmly, trying to quiet the distraught man. "What seems to be her trouble?"

"I don't know." His voice broke. "We thought it was just a cold when she got up this morning, so we kept her home from school. But she kept getting worse and worse."

Mrs. Orlis turned to Carl. "I'm going over with Glen and see if there's anything I can do," she said.

Carl Orlis nodded. He knew what was going to happen the minute Glen said his little girl was ill.

"I may have to stay all night, so don't worry about me if I don't come back until morning."

She kissed him and Danny good-bye and went out with Glen.

"I know Mother hated to leave tonight, Danny," his dad said, "with you just getting here and everything, but the people around here seem to depend on her for emergencies like this."

"I understand." A grin creased Danny's young

face. "It seems like old times for sure. That's one of the best things I remember about Mom. She's always going somewhere to help someone."

"That's the thing everybody remembers most about Mom," Carl said.

* * * *

In Fairview that night Jim Morgan went over to see Connie McCloud.

"I've been trying to call you," he said, "but the phone's been busy or you haven't been at home."

"I'm sorry, Jim, but you know how busy we are with Fritz in the hospital."

He paused a moment.

"I thought maybe you'd found another boyfriend who was crowding me out."

"I've had plenty of chances, if that's what you mean."

Hurt leaped to his eyes.

"It's sure not what I want. I can tell you that much."

"You don't have to worry," she replied. "Nobody can take your place."

Jim grinned broadly. "That's what I wanted to hear. Let's go back to the house and pop some corn."

"That sounds like a wonderful idea."

Back in the McCloud house Jim helped Connie fix the popcorn.

"It sure is good to be with you again, Connie," he said. "It's been such a long time."

She nodded. "That's what I keep telling myself," she replied. "I like it at State a lot. If you were only going to school there too, everything would be perfect."

He glanced at her obliquely. "Or, if you were just going to CBI," he countered, "everything would be perfect."

Briefly silence reigned between them. It was as though a barrier, that had been invisible before, had suddenly been revealed to both of them.

"I've really enjoyed getting your letters, Jim," Connie said, at last. "I don't mind telling you, the mailbox is the first place I go when I finish my eleven o'clock class. And if I've got a letter from you, my day is made."

He laughed. "My roommate accuses me of spending more time at the mailbox than the people who sort the mail."

"I'm glad," she murmured, more to herself than to him. "It makes me feel good to know that my letters mean so much to you."

It was a minute or two before he spoke again. But when he did, he changed the subject abruptly.

"Connie, in your letters you have never mentioned what church you're going to."

She colored delicately.

"Well, I–"

He waited.

"I–I–" She laughed her embarrassment. "Oh, I guess I'd just as well confess. I haven't gone to church very often since school started last September."

Jim focused his gaze intently on her. There was concern in his eyes, but he did not condemn her.

"I'm sorry about that, Connie," he said, quietly. "I'm terribly sorry."

"You don't understand." Her voice rose defensively. "In our dorm everybody is out late on Saturday night so it's only natural that we sleep in."

"*Everybody* is out late on Saturday night?" he echoed. In spite of himself, jealousy stole into his voice.

"Well, almost everybody. And they all sleep in, so there isn't anyone to go with."

His gaze did not leave hers.

"One of the fellows who was pressuring me to go to State last spring said I wouldn't have to worry about not having a car to get to church," he told her. "He said a number of churches picked up kids every Sunday and took them out to services. And some-times I guess they took them to dinner afterward, too. At least that's what he said."

"I–I guess they do." She squirmed uncomfortably. "But I–I sort of got out of the habit, I guess." Her gaze met his. "But that doesn't mean I'm letting my Christian standards slip. I still believe exactly the same as I did before I went away."

Jim did not press the subject further, but he was as disturbed as ever when he went back home after spending the evening with Connie. There was some-thing about her that was changed. She seemed to be indifferent to her own spiritual needs.

* * * *

Mary Orlis did not come back home that night. Danny and his dad got up the next morning, fixed breakfast, and had devotions together. When they finished, Danny pushed back from the table and got to his feet.

"Well, it's quit snowing," he said. "I suppose I'd better get out and see what I can do to get that aircraft to flying."

"Want me to help?" his dad asked.

The missionary pilot shook his head. "Thanks, Dad, but I don't think there's much you can do." He pulled on his parka. "Have you got a snow shovel?"

"Now there's something I know how to use better than you do," Carl said firmly. "I'll scoop out the plane while you go to work on the engine."

Danny paused. He didn't really want his dad to go over and start scooping. Yet he knew that it was useless for him to protest. Besides, it would be good for them to work together the way they used to do.

The wind had gone down, but the clouds were still dark and foreboding. And now and then a few new flakes of snow drifted aimlessly about – mute evidence that it could start to snow again at any moment.

Carl Orlis set to work with the snow shovel, pacing himself carefully, while Danny broke out his tool kit and set to work on the engine. They had only been there a few minutes when he saw a dark figure hurrying toward them across the snow.

"It looks as though we're going to have company, Dad," he said.

Carl Orlis looked up.

"Why, it's Glen. I wonder what he's doing over this way so early in the morning."

"His little girl must be worse."

The newcomer was panting so heavily when he reached them that they could scarcely understand him.

"Danny!" he cried. "You've got to fly Carol down to Warroad right away!"

The pilot glanced at the ailing engine.

"I'll fly her to Warroad as soon as I can," he said, "but I'll have to fix the engine first. I had to make a forced landing last night."

"But you've got to go now!" Glen exclaimed irrationally. "She'll die, if you don't!"

"Now, wait a minute," Carl broke in calmly. "Just exactly what's wrong with Carol?"

"Mary says she's got a terrible case of pneumonia. She can hardly breathe. We've got to get her to a hospital fast."

"Danny's working on the engine now, Glen. He'll have it just as soon as he can."

The girl's father was so distraught he scarcely knew what he was saying.

"But we can't wait for anything! We've got to go now! She's going to die if we don't!"

CHAPTER 11

PLANE REPAIRED

Thoughtfully, Danny turned from the engine, a wrench in his hand.

"I know just how you feel, Glen," he said. "I'd probably be the same way if she was my little girl."

"What do you know about it?" The man's lips curled bitterly about the words. "Carol's not your daughter! She's mine! And she's going to die if she doesn't get down to Warroad to the hospital right away."

Carl Orlis went over to the frantic young man.

"Glen," he said, soothingly, "why don't you go back home and tell Mary that Danny's working on the engine? Tell her that he's doing everything he can to get the engine repaired and as soon as he does, he'll take Carol to Warroad."

Glen stared from Carl to Danny and back again, wild-eyed and trembling.

"I'm not leaving here until you've got this thing

ready to go into the air!" He grabbed Danny's arm roughly. "We can't let her lie there until she dies! Don't you understand? We've got to do something!"

"Then stop this sort of thing!" Danny ordered sternly. "And let me get to work!"

There was a brief silence.

"What's the matter with it? Is it something you can fix here?" Glen's voice was harsh with emotion.

"There's something wrong with the carburetor heat," Danny explained. "It iced up on me coming in."

A strange look gleamed in Glen's eyes.

"Then it will fly!" he exclaimed.

"As long as the carburetor doesn't ice up again, it will fly," Danny said. "But that's a big 'if' this time of year."

Glen's mouth narrowed to a firm hard fine. "Then you're going to get this engine started and get it started right now!" he ordered. "And as soon as I can get back with Carol we're going to take off!"

Danny shook his head. "We can't risk that, Glen. We've got to get the carburetor heat fixed first."

"We'll take a chance on not needing it."

Danny maintained his composure, but his voice was firm and unyielding.

"But I don't take chances when it comes to flying."

"You'd rather take chances with my little girl's life, is that it?" he cried.

"No, that isn't it. Now, if you'll just go away and leave me alone, I'll get this fixed as soon as I can so we can fly. I'm telling you now for the last time. We're not going to take off until this aircraft is operating properly."

Glen's face whitened and anger flashed in his dark eyes. "What kind of a man are you, anyway?"

Danny did not answer him. Instead, he turned to his father.

"Dad, why don't you hand that shovel to Glen and let him finish scooping the plane out. You can go back and get Mom, Mrs. Rehfield and the little girl and bring them to our house. That way we won't lose any time in getting in the air once we get the repairs made."

Carl Orlis started to protest, but Danny nodded significantly at the newcomer.

"Maybe that would be a good idea, at that," he said.

Glen Rehfield snatched up the shovel and began to throw snow furiously. Danny watched him for an instant or two before turning back to the airplane engine. He knew exactly how the girl's father felt. He had felt that same way himself in the face of serious illness.

Without stopping work Danny prayed in silence for the sick girl, and that God would help him get the plane repaired so he could fly her to Warroad in time for the doctor to cure the pneumonia that gripped her.

Having something to do seemed to relieve some of Glen's anxiety. He worked as rhythmically as a machine, throwing shovelful after shovelful of snow. He drew back the big scoop, jabbed it savagely into the drift, and threw the snow to one side. There were no breaks in his motion, no stopping for rest until he finally moved the last of the snow around the little plane. Once that was accomplished he hurried to the front of the aircraft where Danny was still working.

"How're you coming?" he demanded. "Will you have it done soon?"

"It shouldn't take too long."

"I'll go get Carol and Sally!"

"Better let them stay in a warm house until we're ready to leave."

Glen Rehfield kept talking to Danny, but the pilot only half heard him as he worked. At last, he finished.

"There! That ought to do it!"

"You mean you've got it fixed?" For the first time hope gleamed in Glen's eyes.

Danny nodded. "Now we've got to put the engine tent on and get some heat under it to warm the motor up enough to turn over."

Anguish tinged Glen Rehfield's voice. "I don't believe you're ever going to get this thing in the air!"

Danny paid no attention to him as he got the canvas engine tent from the aircraft, shrouded the motor and lit the firepot under it. There was a constant prayer in his heart as he worked, a prayer that the engine would start without difficulty and that flying weather would hold so they could get Carol to Warroad safely.

Glen went hurrying off. By the time the pilot started the engine Glen was back with his wife and daughter on the power toboggan.

"I figured this would save a little time," he said.

Danny helped them get into the plane while the engine idled to warm up. The little girl was desperately ill. He could tell by the flush in her cheeks and the glaze in her soft blue eyes. She was a sweet little thing, with a gentle smile and wide, luminous eyes.

"Are you going to take me to the doctor?" she whispered, so softly he could scarcely hear her.

"That's right. We're going to take you down to Warroad to the doctor so he can fix you up and get you feeling well again."

"Are–are we going in an airplane?"

He nodded. "We're going in an airplane."

There was a long pause. She smiled once more – faintly.

"I always did want to ride in an airplane."

Sally Rehfield was in the back with Carol, and Glen sat beside Danny in front. Danny checked the carburetor heat once more to make sure that it was operating properly and took off.

Glen turned in the seat.

"How do you like this, Carol?" he asked.

"It's fun."

"We'll be in Warroad and have you in the hospital before you–"

The engine sputtered.

"What was that?" the girl's father demanded.

Danny opened the carburetor heat as the motor missed again. In a moment, the roughness in the engine's operation disappeared and it was running smoothly once more.

"What was that?" Glen repeated.

"We were picking up a little carburetor ice, that's all."

"But we haven't been in the air very long," he protested.

"It doesn't take long when conditions are right for icing."

For a minute or two there was a pained silence.

"This makes me feel awfully foolish," Glen said.

Danny did not answer him. He had picked up the radio phone and called Warroad so an ambulance could be waiting for them when they landed. As they nosed down to the airport, they saw the big vehicle pulled up beside the little building.

"They're here," Danny said. "You'll be in the hospital in a few minutes, Carol."

While the ambulance attendants were loading Carol in the big vehicle Glen Rehfield turned to Danny.

"Thanks, fella," he said, thrusting out his hand.

"That's all right. I'm only glad I was able to help." Glen hesitated, forming words in his mind.

"If you hadn't fixed that carburetor heat before we took off at the Angle, we'd have been in real trouble, wouldn't we?"

Danny nodded. "We would have been in trouble, all right. But we don't have to think about that. It was fixed before we took off."

"I know, but that was no thanks to me. I was so upset about Carol all I could think about was getting her on the way. I didn't realize what could have happened if we'd taken a chance. I'm glad you didn't let me stampede you into doing something foolish."

* * * *

Danny went back to Angle Inlet to pick up his parents. On the way south he radioed the Warroad airport and asked how Carol Rehfield was getting along.

"Hang on. I'll call the hospital and check. Over."

"Roger. Standing by. Over."

A moment or two later the answer came.

"They say she's a mighty sick little girl, but the doctor doesn't anticipate any difficulty now that he has her in the hospital. Over."

"Thank God."

"What did you say?" There was a strange tone in the airport manager's voice.

"I said thank God that she's going to be all right. Over."

"Oh." There was a long silence. "That's what I thought you said. Over and out."

Danny repeated the news to his folks.

"That's wonderful!" his mother exclaimed.

* * * *

Danny and Kay planned an open house for his folks' thirtieth wedding anniversary. So many people expressed interest in coming that they weren't sure they would have room for everyone. Mary and Carl Orlis were astonished by the response.

"I can't understand it, Kay," Mrs. Orlis said. "I thought this was just going to be a little family affair. I didn't have any idea anyone else would want to come."

"It started out to be a little family affair," Kay said, laughing pleasantly. "But we soon found out that you had a lot of friends here."

Mrs. Orlis shook her head. "I can't understand it," she repeated. "Why would all these people want to come to our anniversary? We hardly know them."

There was a long silence.

"I can tell you why they want to come, Mother."

Kay said seriously. "They've heard us tell what kind of people you and Dad are – how you've lived for the Lord and how your lives have honored Him. They want to come and honor you on your wedding anniversary and to get acquainted with you."

Carl Orlis broke in. "We haven't really done anything for the Lord, Kay. We've often wished that we could have gone to Bible school and prepared ourselves so we could really have served Him." He paused thoughtfully. "One of the real regrets of my life has been that I haven't been able to win more people for Christ."

Kay sat down beside Danny's father and put her hand on his. "Dad, your life has been a testimony for Christ ever since you and Mother moved up on the Angle. I don't think you know how many people you've been a testimony to, or how many you've helped."

Danny nodded. "That's right, Dad," he said. "When I think of the example you've been to me, and to Ron, Roxie, and Jim, I can begin to see just exactly what a strong testimony for Christ can accomplish. And I know we're only a few of those you've influenced."

Carl Orlis coughed and got to his feet.

"Well, if our Christian testimony has been of help to someone, both Mother and I are very happy. But there's one thing to remember, 'To God be the glory.'"

CHAPTER 12

AUNT CARMEN IS TROUBLED

The Davis triplets had been writing regularly to their Aunt Carmen and their cousins, but Mrs. Roper did not show the letters to her husband. There was no particular reason for letting him see them, she told herself. They were typical letters from typical kids. They wrote about school and what they were doing with Danny and Kay. There was nothing in them Clarence could have taken exception to unless he got mad because they wrote about Sunday school and church and the Bible verses that they were learning. Clarence was a violent man as far as religion was concerned, but he was also reasonable. It wouldn't be like him to lose his temper over such little things.

Still, she knew about the time when DeeDee, Doug, and Del were due to write, and she managed to work things out so she would be the one to get the mail on those days. When there happened to be a letter from them, she read it at the mailbox and sneaked it into the house to an upstairs dresser drawer.

Almost invariably a letter from the triplets meant a sleepless night for Carmen. She would lie in bed wide-eyed and staring, trying to do battle against the ache in her heart.

Her fiery temper flared.

They did that sort of thing purposely, she told herself. They wrote about all the things they did at church just to aggravate her. Well, she was just as good as they were, even though she didn't go to church or profess to be a Christian. She didn't care what they thought.

Quietly, to keep from waking Clarence, she swung her feet over the side of the bed and sat up. Her shoulders trembled and her hands were working nervously.

This wasn't the doing of the triplets, she reasoned as she sat alone in the darkness, thinking. Somebody else was behind those letters. Somebody who was trying to get her to make a fool of herself over religion the same as they did.

And it wasn't difficult to figure out who was behind it, she thought inwardly. Danny and Kay Orlis had the same warped ideas about religion that her sister and that missionary husband of hers had. They probably would think they were doing something for Rosalita by getting the kids to write to her that way.

What was it they called it?

She thought for a moment.

Witnessing!

Well, she'd show them whether their witnessing did any good or not. She'd write them a letter that would sizzle all the way to Minnesota. She'd let them know that they might as well quit it. They weren't getting anywhere with tactics like that.

Then the pain came back again in great, surging blows. Carmen had never felt this way when Rosalita had tried to talk with her about the sin in her life and her need for a Savior. She'd gotten angry, told her off, and changed the subject. She and Clarence laughed about it afterward. It was a sort of family joke for years. It had bothered Rosalita and Jerry a great deal more than it had ever bothered her.

Reluctantly Carmen slipped back into bed, knowing as she did so that the irate letter to Danny and Kay Orlis would never be written.

She was still vaguely disturbed as she went about her housework the next morning. It had been weeks since she had been so uneasy. Actually, she reasoned inwardly, the letter from the triplets had been innocent enough. They simply wrote to her about the things they were doing the same as she did when she wrote to them. They probably didn't think anything about it.

Then why did it disturb her so?

She was still pondering that when she opened Phil's bedroom door.

He started suddenly.

"Mom!" he cried.

She glared at him.

"What are you doing?"

"I–I–" The words trailed helplessly off into space.

"Phil, your dad would skin you alive if he saw you reading a Bible." She was surprised at the concern, the lack of anger in her voice. It was almost as though she approved. "If Dad had opened this door instead of me, he'd give you a good beating."

"I know." The boy answered simply, as though it was a risk he had to take.

Mechanically, Carmen moved to the desk and touched her son's Bible with the tip of her forefinger.

"You promised Dad you wouldn't have anything more to do with that religion, Phil," she said, trying to be as firm as she knew her husband would want her to be.

He shook his head. "He asked me not to, Mom, but I didn't promise him. I couldn't do that. You see, I'm a Christian now."

She picked up the Bible gingerly, as though it was some forbidden object that might harm her in the touching.

"Are–are you going to tell him, Mom?" There was fright in the boy's young voice.

"That depends." Her gaze met his. "Are you going to keep reading it, or aren't you?"

The silence was deafening.

"Don't you see, Mom?" he exclaimed in desperation. "I–I have to!"

She turned quickly and stormed away.

No, she didn't see! She didn't see at all! That was the trouble! There were so many things she couldn't understand – so many emotions that surged within her. Emotions she had never before felt in her life.

She was still trembling when her husband came into the kitchen some minutes later.

"Carmen!" He hurried over to her. "What's the matter? What's wrong?"

"Nothing." She managed a weak little laugh. Nothing at all."

"Now I know better. What is it?"

"Nothing really." She went over to the kitchen table and sat down. "I was just thinking about the triplets, that's all."

The lie burned in her throat, but it seemed to satisfy her rancher husband. He pulled out a chair and sat down across from her.

"I might've known it was something like that," he said. "I suppose you'd like to have 'em back."

She shook her head.

"We can't. We signed them away legally."

"I guess that's right." He thought for a moment or two in silence. "If you're so lonesome for 'em, why don't you go up to Minnesota for a few days and see how they're making out? That might make you feel a lot better."

Carmen's cheeks blanched. Go up there? He didn't know what he was saying. She couldn't go where Danny and Kay Orlis and the triplets could talk to her about religion. She wouldn't dare!

"No!" she almost shouted the word.

Clarence laughed. "Take it easy, will you? You don't

have to get so shook up about it. I just suggested that you go up and see them. You don't have to. It doesn't make any difference to me whether you do or not. Actually, I couldn't care less, one way or the other."

He reached out clumsily and patted her hand.

"You must think I'm getting to be some charac-ter if you start thinking I'm going to make you do things you don't want to do." His manner softened. "You ought to know me better than that, Carmen. I bark a lot, but I don't bite."

She wrapped her tiny hands about his gnarled fingers.

"I'm sorry, Clarence. I know you're not that way at all. And I wouldn't want you any different than you are right now."

He sighed with mock relief. "That's better. That's a lot better. I sure wasn't aimin' to start changing. I can tell you that much."

He got to his feet and kissed her.

"I don't want to hear any more of this nonsense about those kids," he went on. "If you want to see them, OK, go and see them. Stay for a week or two and get it out of your system. If you don't, that's OK too. Only don't let yourself get worked up about them. You hear me?"

She nodded wordlessly.

Carmen had plenty of work to do, but for a long while after Clarence went outside, she remained motionless at the kitchen table.

She had lied to him. For the first time since she could remember, she had lied to him. She felt terrible.

Phil came down after a few minutes, as though nothing had happened between the two of them.

"Bye, Mom." With that he headed out the door.

"Where are you going?" she called after him.

"Out to ride fence for Dad."

She stared after him until he disappeared. Phil was different, she had to admit. She wasn't quite ready to admit that it was the triplets' religion that had changed him. Maybe he was just growing up and getting a little more mature and responsible. But whatever it was, he was becoming a lot more like the son both she and Clarence wanted him to be.

* * * *

Back in Fairview Del and Doug sat on either side of Carl Orlis. "Tell us about this crow Danny had when he was a boy, will you, Uncle Carl?" Doug asked.

"Could he really talk?" Del put in.

"He not only could talk, he could sound exactly like Danny's mother calling him. The truth is, there were times when Danny couldn't tell them apart."

As he related incidents about the talking crow Danny used to have DeeDee and Jill moved closer. Even Kent, who was listening to a football game on the radio, turned it down so he could hear.

Danny saw what was going on and glanced at his mother and Kay.

"It looks as though Dad's got himself an attentive audience," he said.

Mrs. Orlis nodded. "I don't think he's enjoyed himself so much since you and Ron were young."

Kay lowered her voice to a whisper. "Look at Kent in there taking it all in. Have you noticed the change in him since he's been home this time?"

Danny nodded. "You wouldn't even know he's the same fellow."

"I was talking with Dad about him last night," Kay said. "He's made a tremendous adjustment to being blind. I don't think he feels sorry for himself at all. And that's so important if he's going to live a happy, purposeful life."

Mrs. Orlis smiled.

"That's all very true, but the thing that has impressed me about him more than anything else has been his spiritual growth. I'll never forget what he was like when we came here to visit you after you first took him and Jill."

"Knowing that he's putting his trust in the Lord and is such a happy Christian makes it a lot easier for me to see him in the condition he's in," Danny said.

Kay nodded. "His life had its effect on Jill, too. She's much more interested in Christ now than she was before."

In the living room, Carl Orlis finally wearied of telling stories. "That's the last one. Now you'd all better take off for bed."

Kent spoke up. "How about having devotions tonight before we go to bed, Uncle Carl?"

Carl eyed him curiously.

"We already had our Bible reading this evening," he said.

"I know, but we always have a time of Bible reading and prayer just before we go to bed – at least, I do. So, I thought it would be a good idea if we did it together tonight, just for a change."

"That sounds fine to me." Carl Orlis reached for his Bible but changed his mind. "You've got your Braille gospel of John along, haven't you, Kent?"

"Sure thing." The boy's young face brightened. "Do you want me to read?"

"That's what I had in mind – that is if you'd like to."

"Oh, sure." He started to get to his feet, but Jill beat him to it.

"I'll get it for you, Kent."

She scampered off. In a minute or two she was back with the book which she laid on her brother's lap. Kent opened it with experienced fingers and began to read John 14.

" 'Let not your heart be troubled: ye believe in God, believe also in me…. ' " There was a tone in his voice that Danny had never heard before – a tone of adoration.

When the Bible reading and prayer were over, Doug and Del went into the bedroom they shared and closed the door behind them.

"That Kent's quite a guy."

"Boy, you can say that again."

"Do you s'pose he really was the kind of a guy he said he was – before he turned his life over to Christ?" Doug wanted to know.

The other boy crossed the room slowly. "Danny said he was a tough one. He used to smoke and lie and everything."

"He's sure not that way anymore."

Doug untied his shoes and kicked them off. He had never talked with a fellow like Kent before.

"Y'know what he told me this afternoon?"

His brother shook his head.

"Nope."

"He said he's glad he's blind."

Del gasped. "What?"

"That's what he said. He told me that the chances are he never would have turned his life over to Christ if he hadn't had that accident and lost his eyesight."

Del thought about that momentarily.

"Do you think he really meant it?"

"I don't know, but he sure sounded as though he did."

Del reached over and touched the Bible on his desk.

"That makes me feel as though my faith isn't anything at all."

There was a short silence.

"I've been getting sort of careless about having my devotions," he went on. "But if a guy like Kent who can't see can do it every day, I sure ought to be able to."

Doug nodded. "And we ought to do something about studying, too. It sure isn't much of a testimony for a Christian to get grades like we've been getting."

Together they knelt to pray.

CHAPTER 13

HOSPITAL VISITORS

Over at the Orlis home Danny and Kay talked seriously with his folks about staying in Fairview to visit for a time.

"I don't know whether we ought to or not," Carl said reluctantly. "I'd like to, but we ought to be getting back home to take care of things."

"But, Dad," Danny protested, "you and Mother haven't been here for a visit in a long time. Now that you're with us, you ought to stay awhile."

Kay went over to her father-in-law's chair. Sitting on the arm, she put her hand on his shoulder.

"Danny won't be flying for a while," she told him. "So he'll be home to visit, too. It would be such a good time for you to stay."

"Well–"

"There really isn't anything you have to do at home, Dad," Danny reminded him. "You told me that yourself."

Carl Orlis turned to his wife. "What do you think, Mother?"

"You already know what I think," she answered. "I told you this morning."

His grin widened.

"I'd just as well have given in right away. I might have known I would lose out."

"Then you'll stay?"

He laughed. "It sounds to me as though I have to. I'm outnumbered."

Impulsively, Kay bent and kissed him.

* * * *

Fritz McCloud had been counting the days until he would be released from the hospital. Although he had been asking the doctor about it every time he saw him, he was surprised when Dr. Walsh told him that he could go home the next day.

"Do you really mean it?" he asked incredulously.

Dr. Walsh frowned. "Of course, if you don't want to go home, Fritz, I'll try to make arrangements for you to stay here a little longer. I think I can manage it."

"You don't need to bother!" he exclaimed, his eyes sparkling.

The doctor reached out and tapped him on the shoulder. "I've been trying and trying to find a reason to keep you, but I can't come up with any, so I'd better leave orders for you to be dismissed in the morning."

Fritz leaned back in his bed and closed his eyes. It was going to be great to go home. He had been looking forward to it ever since the pain in his leg went away. It would be good to be out of the hospital and to get to school and church again, and to see all the kids.

He missed going to church as much as he missed being at home. It would be great to sing in the choir once more and to hear the pastor's messages. He was able to get them on the radio, but being in church was different.

Fritz opened his eyes momentarily. Connie would be home from school again before long. He was glad for that and for the fact that he would be home and could make an opportunity to talk with her.

Somehow, he was concerned about his older sister. Her letters were interesting and nice enough. They didn't indicate that she was doing anything at State that she shouldn't, or that her convictions on separation were weakening. Yet, they were disturbing. They indicated a certain carelessness toward the things of God – little things that meant nothing in themselves but taken together evidenced a subtle change in her attitude toward Christ.

Silently he prayed that God would make her see that only a total committal of her life was pleasing to Him.

He was still praying when the door opened, and Alex and Robin Smith came into his room. Fritz opened his eyes quickly.

"Hi." His entire being brightened at the sight of the one-time Fairview football star. "It's great to see you!"

"You're looking great, Fritz," Alex said.

He and Robin pulled up chairs and sat down.

"I'm doing great." His grin broadened. "And what's more, I get to go home tomorrow."

Robin's lips parted as though to speak, but she hesitated momentarily. Finally, she voiced her thoughts. "Alex has been so concerned about your injury that he insisted on coming up here to see you as soon as we got home from school this weekend."

Her young husband nodded. "I'll say I've been concerned." The grin was gone from his face. "A knee injury like you had can take a fellow out of football for life."

Fritz nodded. "Maybe you think I haven't been doing some thinking about that myself."

"What have they found out?" Alex asked. "Do they think your leg's going to be OK?"

Fritz shook his head.

"They don't know for sure. Dr. Walsh told me that it'll be several months before they'll know about my knee."

The college boy drew in a long breath. "That's tough," he said. "If it had happened to me, I don't think I could take it."

Fritz' grin was infectious. "I love playing football and all of that, but I don't have to play football to be happy. I have the Lord Jesus Christ."

Alex's eyes widened, but he did not reply.

"Christ is the One who gives direction and purpose to my life. He's the One who makes me happy. Just to know that I'm on my way to heaven and that

He will help me through times like this – or worse – makes everything a lot easier for me.”

Alex shook his head incredulously.

“But I don’t mind telling you,” Fritz went on, “that I’m not giving up yet. I’m going to keep plugging away. And if there’s any chance for me to play again, I’m going to.”

Robin broke in quickly. “I think it’s wonderful to have faith like that, Fritz,” she said. “And I’m sure the Lord is going to honor it. I’m going to be praying for you.”

When Robin and Alex left the hospital room half an hour or so later, Alex was still scowling.

“That character!” His lips curled. “Who does he think he’s kidding?”

“He’s not trying to kid anyone,” Robin said. “That’s exactly what he believes. That’s what I’ve been trying to tell you that Christ could mean to you, Alex. He can make you happier than you’ve ever been in your life.”

Anger twisted Alex’s youthful face and his eyes snapped.

“Lay off, will you? How many times do I have to tell you that I’m not buying that religion of yours? I don’t care how hard you push.”

Suddenly he stopped and faced her. “I’ll bet you had that deal all set up, didn’t you?”

She stared at him. “What do you mean?”

“You had him all primed to give me the needle when I talked to him about his knee, didn’t you?”

Tears clung to Robin’s eyelids.

"What do you mean?"

"You wanted him to preach to me, didn't you?"

"No, I didn't, Alex. Honest. I didn't even know you wanted to come over here until a little while ago."

Slowly the anger in his eyes faded away.

"I guess that's right." He paused briefly. "But lay off this religion kick of yours, OK?"

Robin choked back a sob. She had been so thrilled when Alex wanted to go and see Fritz. It had seemed an answer to prayer. But that wasn't the way it turned out at all.

* * * *

In the hospital room Fritz closed his eyes momentarily. He didn't know whether his brief testimony had done any good as far as Alex was concerned, but he was thankful for the opportunity. It was wonderful the way God was providing him with chances to witness. He had been able to talk with Dr. Walsh, a couple of nurses, a cleaning lady, and several fellows on the football team who came up to see him. Now he had been able to say a word to Alex about what Christ had done for him.

Fritz began to thank God for the opportunities to testify that He had given. Actually, he had been able to talk to more and different people since he had been hurt than he had before. His heart was so full of joy he didn't think he could contain it all.

God was good!

THE DANNY ORLIS SERIES

The Danny Orlis series, by Bernard Palmer, delivers a blend of adventure, mystery, and suspense through various settings—from the Canadian wilderness to Guatemalan jungles. Danny Orlis, an adept outdoorsman, skilled athlete, and committed Christian, employs his quick thinking, calm bravery, and biblical solutions to confront everyday problems and hair-raising dangers. Early stories focus on Danny navigating school life, sports, and outdoor challenges, while in later books, Danny and his wife Kay provide wisdom and guidance to youngsters facing lifelike situations and challenges. Having sold over two million copies, this series has made Palmer a renowned author in Christian youth literature. Palmer is also the author of the Felicia Cartright series and various other series for Christian youth.

AVAILABLE FROM WWW.ANEKOPRESS.COM

www.ingramcontent.com/pod-product-compliance
Lightning Source LLC
Chambersburg PA
CBHW060502300726
48975CB00008B/2609